RAVENSGILL

Other books by William Mayne

RAVENSGILL

by WILLIAM MAYNE

E. P. DUTTON & CO., INC. NEW YORK

First published in the U.S.A. 1970 by E. P. Dutton & Co.
Copyright © 1970 by William Mayne

SBN: 0-525-38081-7 (Trade)   SBN: 0-525-38082-5 (DLLB)
Library of Congress Catalog Card Number: 70-81721
Printed in the U.S.A.
First Edition

TO HANNAH

I

"WHAT'S GRAN tapping for?" said Mother. She was bending over to draw the kettle off the fire, and looking up at the ceiling of the kitchen at the same time, because Gran was above the ceiling lying in bed. The kettle handle was hot, and Mother put out her tongue.

"Use a cloth," said Judith. "She's tapping away to get Mick out of bed, but he was out of bed before she was awake."

"Then what have you been doing getting the cows in?" said Mother, mostly with her tongue out still as she poured boiling water into the teapot, holding the kettle by a small part of its handle. "Where's Mick?"

"I'll tell him breakfast's ready," said Judith. "I sort of know where he is." She pulled a wellington boot back on to the foot that had just lost it and went out of the kitchen.

"Tell the little ones too," said Mother. "I can hear them."

The two little ones were along the side of the house. They had two dog chains joined together, with one end on the ring in the wall. One little one was swinging the chain and the other was skipping, and they were both singing, or chanting, loudly, "High, low, dolly, pepper," with less and less breath each time, but just as much noise. "Pepper" was usually followed by a scream, because at that word the chain was swung at

7

double speed, and the skipper was not quick enough to avoid having her knees rattled.

Judith took a skip over the high end of the chain, and told them both to go in for breakfast. She went on beyond the end of the house to the edge of the field and looked down into the valley. This morning there was a mist, with the sunshine lying along it and casting shadows on the thick air. The pine tree that stood alone at the bottom of the field looked as if it were racing along trailing its own movement, like a drawing. Down the valley the mist grew brighter until it was the sun. Opposite, the hillside hung a green gold. Up the valley, to the right, the mist began to thin; and over it there lay the long shelf, from side to side of the valley, that was the top of the dam, with turrets at the end and clock-like knob in the middle, so that it looked like a giant's mantelpiece laid down by some playing giant child.

Judith barked Mick's name into the mist. It barked back at her, from the giant mantelpiece, or perhaps from the part of the dam below the mist, where it stood out of the floor of the valley and sealed it up.

After the echo Mick's voice sounded, from not far away. Then he was over the wall, and coming up for his breakfast.

"Still echoing," said Judith, listening up the valley.

"It does," said Mick; but he was not interested any more in echoes. Judith gave another shout to the hills, and did not wait for the answer, but walked back to the house with Mick.

The last of the cows came out of the shippon into the field, listened to the echo, and took no more notice of it than Mick had. They looked down the other way, into the mist, where there was the sound of the mail van coming up the track. It was hidden, and then it was a red glow, and then it was a dry appearance in the dry yard, turning round busily before stopping.

Daddy came out of the top door of the shippon. There was a rattling of milk-can lids behind him, and then Wig followed, wiping his old hands on his fixed knees.

The postman got out of his van with the letters in his hand, and walked into the kitchen. He always had a cup of tea here, because New Scar House was his most distant call. He had more deliveries to make, but they were all as he went home. "Now then, Mrs Chapman," he said, to Mother; and he nodded to Gran, who had come down to sit by the fire. He knew her name, Mrs Oldersby, but he had never used it. Gran did not think much of postmen who came in a van: in her young days the postmen had walked. Then they had deserved cups of tea.

The postman put the letters on the table and drank his tea. He drank it very hot, and then went, leaving dust in the mist and a heap of blue smoke swirling in the yard.

Judith ran upstairs and took off her cow-herding clothes and put on school uniform. Mick was in the next room muttering to himself, which meant he was tying his tie. When they came down breakfast was on the table, Daddy and Wig were drying their hands on the roller towel, the two little ones were dipping bread and butter in the dish of bacon, and Gran was saying that she wouldn't have any bacon, thank you, at my age, let the bairns have it.

Daddy took his share of the bacon and forked some into his mouth, following it with a lump of bread and a gulp of tea. While the mixture was being chewed he looked at the letters. Some he put to one side, the farm business letters. One he

9

handed to Mother. It was from the Women's Institute of another village.

"Why, Wig," said Daddy. "Is it your birthday?"

"Another two months," said Wig. "Not while August."

"But someone's sent you a letter," said Daddy, handing it over to him.

"Well, there," said Wig. "Maybe my brother sending a present early." He wiped his knife on his bread, and cut the envelope along the top and pulled the letter out. Then he had to shuffle in his pocket for his glasses, polish them on his elbow, and lift them to his nose. Then he unfolded the letter and read it through.

"Nay," he said. "At last. She . . ." Then he read the letter again, folded it, put it in the envelope, and put the envelope in his pocket, took off his glasses, put them in the case that was so old it was pure shiny metal, not cloth.

"That policeman's dead," he said. "The one that was after your Lizzie that time. That was a bit since."

"Who was Lizzie?" said Judith. "And why wouldn't she have him?"

"It wasn't that way on," said Wig. "He was trying to get summat proved against her, but he never could; and he was waiting on and waiting on until she stepped wrong, but she never did."

"That's enough, Wig," said Mother very sharply, getting up from her place and going to Gran. Gran had not said anything, or moved. She had been sipping tea when Wig spoke, and she had turned her head to look at him, and gone on looking, and forgotten the cup in her fingers. The cup had tipped, her hand had drooped, and tea was pouring into the butter, washing it oily away on to the cloth. Mother took the cup. Gran turned her head.

"I am startled," she said. "I am. But no worse than that, so you need fuss me no more, Margaret. Lizzie was a bad girl, but I think of her at times. It's a long time since her name was named out. You know there's no one else left that knew her, but only me."

"I did," said Wig. "We were in school together, you and me and her, and my brother and your sister that went abroad, and a lot more too."

"I'll go and sit in the room," said Gran. "Now, just let me go, I can walk, there's no need to help me." She shook away Mother's helping arm, and walked out of the kitchen into the room, closed the door behind her and sat down in the chair that squeaked. They heard her.

"Now, Wig," said Daddy. "That's unsettled her."

Wig looked at his plate. "Maybe there's some more tea," he said, holding up his cup.

"Who was Lizzie?" said Judith again. "What did she do?"

"You be quiet," said Mick. "And it's nearly time to go."

"I didn't ask you," said Judith. "I asked Daddy."

It was Mother that answered. "Lizzie was your Gran's cousin."

"She is yet," said Wig.

"There was some trouble about fifty years ago," said Mother. "We don't think about it any more. All right?"

"Aye," said Judith, "but..."

"You heard," said Daddy.

"Don't be so fond," said Mick. So Judith dug her heel into his ankle, got up from the table, took up her school bag, and walked out of the house. No one stopped her. It was time to go in any case.

During breakfast the mist had melted. Already the walls of the house and of the farm buildings were sending back warmth. A small different mist was coming off the meadows, where the sun was drying the grass. The little mist was from the dew, rising a foot and then turning to invisible vapour.

The track led downhill a little way, then turned away from where it used to run and went to the end of the dam and crossed the valley along the top of it. The old road was a mark on the field now, leading nowhere.

Judith marched at first, hoping that Mick would come after her, so that she could kick his ankle again, but much harder. These days, she thought, Mick was not such a good brother, now he was just about to leave school. Then she stopped marching and slowed to a walk, because she was out early and there was no hurry.

She was first at the top of the dam, first and alone. There was no one to see or hear, to be seen or to be heard. On her right was the shrunk water at its summer level, ahead was the straight and narrow road across the dam, and to her left the valley falling down to the tiny river among the trees. The far water hurried and tripped, a bird on the bank chipped a song on two notes, and on the moor behind the pewits linked their songs together in a silver chain.

There was a ringing of bicycle bells, and Mick came along like the tall mother bird of some noisy breed on his bicycle, trailing behind him the two little ones on tricycles. Mick was leading Judith's bicycle for her.

All four of them rode gently across the level top of the dam.

They could see only ahead, because the walls either side were too high. It was like being in a topless tunnel. By pedalling along in the right mood it was possible to think that you were standing still yourself, and that the hillside ahead was merely getting larger, not nearer.

Then they came out on to the rough track again, by the gate. The school taxi was bumbling up the road, bouncing in the corrugations. The road here had been a railway line when the dam was being built. The rails and the sleepers had been lifted, but the ballast was still there, ridge and hollow all the way, because no one had flattened it yet.

They put their bicycles behind the gate, and waited for the taxi. There was no point in going to meet it because it had to come up here to turn round before going back to the village. The two little ones stayed in the village for their school, and Judith and Mick caught the bus down the dale. It was three miles from farm to village, and the taxi came twice each day for them, fetching and bringing back.

They waited for it. "What was all that with Gran?" said Judith. The little ones were playing with a nettle, so that Judith thought they would be out of the way if Mick had to say anything they should not hear.

"Don't you know?" said Mick.

"Nothing," said Judith. "Nothing at all. Do you?"

"Not really," said Mick. "Not rightly. I'm not right keen to know, if they don't want to say. It'll be summat and nowt, whatever it is, they're so old, Wig and Gran, and it was fifty years ago."

"But there was a policeman," said Judith. "That's more summat than it is nowt. And I didn't know Wig had a brother."

Then the taxi was smoking beside them, and turning, and they got into the back seat, so narrow that they both had to have the little ones on their knees. The little ones were playing a game that involved a great deal of fighting against as many people as possible.

In the afternoon, on the way home, that game had finished, and they were merely making strange noises and shrieks and bouncing.

When they got home Mother said: "Who's going to have a quick tea and then go right down to the village to post a letter?"

"I did the cows this morning," said Judith. "So Mick ought to do both things, but he can't, can he?"

"No, he can't," said Mick. "I'll do the cows and you can do what you like."

There were two letters to post. One was to the Women's Institute, and that was already stamped. The other letter was Gran's, and Gran was now completing it. She was in bed, not ill, or anything like that; but she could think better in bed.

There was one more thing to do on the journey, as she came home, and that was to go up to Applegarth Farm and tell Mrs Spence about the W.I. letter. Mrs Spence was President, and Mother was Secretary.

"Good," said Judith. "When I've been there I'll go on right to the top of the hill and come down on the top road, so it'll be downhill there and downhill back."

Gran's letter came downstairs in its blue envelope. "Don't forget to stamp it," said Mother, stowing both letters away in Judith's blazer pocket, and putting sixpence in with them for the stamp.

It was a vibratory run down to the village. The railway sloped down all the time, though not too steeply. Now and then it was necessary to pedal to keep going. The Post Office was in the old station house. Judith parked the bicycle at the edge of the platform, climbed up, and went into the building and bought the stamp.

The letter to the W.I. had a fold across it, because it was in an envelope that had come ready addressed and stamped. Gran's letter was smooth and smelt of moth-preventer, from being in a drawer. The address was blue as well, but a rich dark blue. Judith wondered whether she had ever seen Gran's writing on anything else but jam labels, saying Raspberry and the date. The letter was to Mrs White, Ravensgill, Garebrough, Yorkshire. Judith dropped both letters in the box.

Then she pulled the bicycle up from the railway, took it out of the station, and climbed up towards Applegarth, pushing the bicycle all the way because of the steepness. She gave her message, and then went on up the hill again, until she was higher up than the farm at home, higher than the dam, and in fact right on the ridge. Here the road turned to the left, and led down the hillside. Judith caught her breath, got on the bicycle, and let herself be pulled down the slope, looking ahead at the silver pool of the reservoir. Judith was aslant the hill, and the reservoir seemed to answer her tilt, tipped among the hills like a fragment of mirror lying on a big bed with several people in peacefully asleep and covered with a brown blanket. Such people could wake, Judith thought; and she put her head down and watched her front wheel.

II

Ravensgill was empty, still, and hot. Water falling down the rocky steps of the valley bottom made a quiet noise that helped to show up the other noises, the bending of grass under small lizards, the ratchet noises of grasshoppers, and the swaying mutter of the wild bees, and the heather stalks lifting again where Bob's foot had trodden them down.

He was up on the edge of the gill, the narrow valley, and the water was far below. The valley went down straight, nicked out of the hillside in one piece, and opened out suddenly into the dale beyond, so that there was a foreground of hill this side, with the house perched on the edge of the gill, and beyond there was the hazy gold turning blue of the opposite side of the dale. Between the near hill and the far hill nothing of the bottom of the dale could be seen.

Bob walked higher, treading on his shadow and wondering whether he could twist it by restraining it with his foot, and perhaps break some of it off; but it was as supple as skin, and got away. A rabbit thumped, and a sheep stamped, and its lambs jumped in the air and pranced back to her.

"Daft besom," said Bob, feeling in his pocket for a calf-nut. The sheep stopped stamping and marked time with its feet, looking carefully at him through the square windows of its eyes.

Then it came to him and took two or three dry and dusty calf-nuts from his hand. The lambs dived under its belly and butted at its udder so heavily that the sheep's back legs left the ground. The sheep walked through them and asked for more nuts, but Bob's pockets were empty.

"There *is* nowt," he said. He sat down at the edge of the gill. The sheep stood by for a little while, and then wandered away. Bob pulled his French book from his pocket. "Je me suis assis," he said in his ordinary voice, and "Je me suis assise," in a high squeaky voice. "Tu t'es assise," he said to the sheep. "But you aren't, you're walking about." The sheep took no notice.

Bob looked back at the French book, tipping the page so that the sunlight was not on it and dazzling him. The firm black mean dead print looked at him blindly and meant nothing. It had less significance than its own pattern. It did not call to mind anything of the language it was in. It only reminded him of school. He looked up from the page, and the lines and spaces of the words printed themselves on what he could see: the far side of the gill and the sky beyond where the sun was free-wheeling down slowly to the west, idly throwing its store of heat heavy on the ground.

Under the same sun, he thought, in other lands, other books were laid out in English with no meaning, and other boys were sitting (ils s'assaient) on a hillside wondering why the book was bigger than the world, like a hand over their eyes.

He put the book down and closed it. In its brown paper wrapper it looked more alive than it did when it was open, promising interest. But opened again it was a dry garden of verse that was not verse.

Bob slid his shoe against the grass. He looked down the gill towards the house. In a little while Dick would be beside the house, shouting and waving, when he wanted the cows sent down for milking. The cows themselves were in the field over the wall, standing in a fan and facing the gate, waiting to be released from the grass. Occasionally one of them would give a despairing shout, and no one would take any notice.

Bob spread himself flat on his back on the slope, holding himself down with his hands to stop himself falling off into space, blue sky above, where an unseeable bird or star sang an insect song; or perhaps it was the thin-threading old echo of the water in the gill coming back attenuated and remote.

He closed his eyes against the mixed dazzle of sight and sound and felt the air darker and warmer upon him, like a blanket, holding him down to the bank he was on.

The French book became large and bright, and opened at a magical page. The words on it sprang out of their places and said themselves, not French, or English, or even pure words, but perhaps more number than word, each with a deep and new meaning that could be understood, if there were time before the next spoke itself.

Bob knew it was a dream, and that he was waking from it as he fell down the bank towards the water without being able to stop, striking himself blow after blow on the rocky sides of the gill, and having his breath thumped from his body on tussocks of grass.

He woke from that dream too, to find that he had not moved from where he had been by even an inch. He sat up, and was not sure whether everything else had moved round him and had only just scrambled back as he woke. He felt that the whole world had shouted at him. But no one had. Not even Dick had appeared by the house. Bob sat with his knees up and his hands on them, and his chin on his hands, and looked muggily at the French book. It looked quite dead now, within and without.

The day just gone at school was in his mind. It had mostly been an ordinary day, with a few laughs, a few sensations of inadequacy, where some master had explained something they already knew but had not bothered to regard as knowledge or useful. Dinner had been that bean stuff, served once a week and ignored once a week. Somebody said that before long, perhaps even before they all left school, the beans would have boiled so many times that they would be at last chewable, if not edible.

There had been a moment of tension during the afternoon. Bob had wondered since, at odd moments, about it. He had wondered two things, whether he should let himself notice that something had come to mind, because it was so trifling a thing; and whether he had accidentally done something wrong and against the honour of the middle school. Members of the staff had praised him for it, but one or two of the next class up had not.

The middle school had been swimming at the baths. The term was more than half done now, and the school was looking for swimmers to go forward to the quarter finals of the secondary school sports for the North Riding. Bob had never thought much about the sports and being in them because Ravensgill was not in the North Riding, but just across the border into the West Riding. However, Garebrough was his nearest school, and he and Dick had both been there.

The people who could hardly swim at all, and merely

splashed about, had been given a little time in the water, and then sent out to dry and dress and come back to watch some selection going on. Bob had been going with them, because he was not interested very much in competing for something he would probably not be allowed to do in the end.

Mr Lankester, though, rubbing his hairy chest with a greyish towel, had blown a lot of greenish baths water from his mouth, shaken back his long forelock of black hair, and said "Hey, White, get back in there."

"West Riding, Sir," said Bob.

"Haven't seen you swim yet," said Mr Lankester, close and loud, and pushing Bob back into the pool. He had immediately blown his whistle, shouted "Everyone out of the water," and slung his towel on the end of the low board so that the corner of it cracked like a whip and damp lint was flicked into the water.

The under-fifteens had gone in first, and been well laughed at for being so ungainly and occasionally sinking or giving up in mid length and swimming to the side, or even walking back and getting out. "Right, right, right, right," said Mr Lankester, writing names on a pad. "You lot go and get changed. Now let's have the next lot, over fifteen under sixteen by the end of term, line up at the end, how many? How Many? HOW MANY?" It is easy to hear a general screaming and shouting, but Mr Lankester's voice was continually lost in the middle reverberations of the roof and the walls and the water and wet ears.

Two heats had been necessary, because there were so many to go. Bob had been in the second lot, and was the first home. Two from each section had been chosen.

"Pretty good, White," said Mr Lankester; and some of the other competitors had thumped him on the back.

The sixteens had gone next, and four were chosen from them. At the end of that heat there were eight boys left, the four fifteen year olds, and the four sixteen year olds. "Just for interest," said Mr Lankester, "you eight swim a length, ready?"

Bob was first of the fifteen year olds. He beat three of the sixteen year olds, and dead-heated the sixteen year old winner, Mick Chapman.

"Everybody out," said Mr Lankester, and they all climbed out, smoothing the water from their hair and pushing each other into the shower.

"Race you back, White," said Mick Chapman, before they got to the shower.

"If you like," said Bob.

"Count together for off," said Mick; and they counted at the edge of the bath. Mr Lankester shouted at them, but they were on the way to the water then, and the next moment it was lightening and supporting them.

Mr Lankester went along the bath beside them, and was waiting for them at the other end. They saw him when they gripped the gutter at the end, standing above them with the water reflecting greenly under his chin.

"I didn't expect that," he said.

"Sorry, Sir," said Mick Chapman. "My idea."

"I didn't expect White to win," said Mr Lankester. "But he did. You'll have to watch your stroke, Chapman, or it won't be you we have in mind for the county championship. You'll both do better with a little attention to detail; but we'll see about that as time goes on."

Then they went to join the queue for the shower. Chapman was put out, Bob knew, but he was not prepared for the touch of spite that followed, when Chapman kicked Bob's towel into the air with a bare foot, and dropped it into the bath while pretending to catch it, and then walked away into his own cubicle. Bob jumped into the bath again and got the towel out, and was shouted at by Mr Lankester for going in without permission, and he had to dry himself on his own shirt. Later he hung the towel to dry in the sun, at school, and somehow it fell down and was tramped into a flower-bed; but Bob could not prove that Chapman had done it, though he was sure of it. No one else heard of these two things. All they knew was that Bob had beaten Chapman in a race, and that there was now competition between them.

The girls in the Fourth Form heard about it, and naturally all took Chapman's side, because they despised the boys in their own form. Only one did not take Mick Chapman's side, because she was his sister Judith; but of course she did not take Bob's either. And so it was forgotten again, in the afternoon mutter of Geography.

Dick came round the end of the farmhouse and shouted up the gill. The cows heard and called back. Bob got up and waved, put the French book in his pocket, and climbed the wall. One or two of the distant cows took small steps forward, as if they had forgotten what they had been standing and waiting for during the last half hour. Bob opened the gate. The leading cows considered whether it was safe to go through the gate, decided it was, and lumbered out into the lane. Bob pushed a red cow out of the way and propped the gate open. Then he went down in front to open the next gate.

Cows and shadows went down the sweet grass lane. Down by the shippon Dick stood and called to them. Bob leaned on the wall by the second gate and watched them pass, then stepped beside the last one, called Minnie, and went down with her with his arm round her neck. She was a gentle cow, but silly, and could get lost when it was impossible to get lost. She was one of the more senior members of the herd, but she had never got very high in rank, and the others pushed her about.

He got her safe to the shippon, and into her stall, and then began to help Dick. There was nothing much to do that would help much, because one person could manage the two milking units easily. It was comfortable, however, to stand in the sun in the doorway with the engine thumping outside and the milk hissing into the units and the row of cow's tails swinging in the dusk of the shippon, and exchange words with whoever was working.

"Where's Tot?" said Bob, as Dick came past.

"Looking at the mower," said Dick answering on his next journey. "Time it was out."

"They've cut some hay further down," said Bob. "I saw."

When the milking was finished Dick started the cooling, and Bob set the cows up the lane, leaving them to find their own way beyond the first gate. Then he came down again to Dick. He was cooling the last of the milk and tipping it into the milk kit.

"Is the Gypsy Queen in?" Bob asked.

"Now Bob," said Dick, mildly, "you haven't to say that."

"I know," said Bob. "But, oh God."

"Oh God," said Dick, shunting up his glasses with the heel of his hand, and echoing Bob. "We'll go in and see."

So they went in, leaving old Tot outside in the dimming light sharpening the blades of the hay-mowing machine.

III

BOB OPENED the house door and let Dick in first.

"Ah, my boys," said Grandma. She was, as usual, doing something unrelated to the need of the moment. She was standing on the table that should have been laid with a meal by now, and she was painting the curtains. Dick looked at the empty table and said something that he hoped would be tactful as well as being reproving.

"Shall we call Tot in for his supper?" he said.

Grandma understood him and resented what he had said. She went on painting for a moment more, getting angry. She had started at the top of the left-hand curtain and was making a tiny pattern of unusual flowers. She had a colour to each brush. On her head she was wearing a cloth that she had painted in stripes a few days ago. On the rest of her she wore an undressed-looking overall she called her housecoat, no stockings, a green sock and a white sock, and a pair of fluffy slippers. She finished a blue flower, then hurled the brush on to the flags of the kitchen floor. It did not dismiss her anger. She dabbed in a yellow centre with the yellow brush, and threw that down, still without regaining her temper, swept in a leaf and threw down the green brush in rage, then threw the red brush across

24

the room so that it clattered among the cups on the dresser. She felt completed at that, and climbed down from the table.

"Where were you thinking of going, then?" she said, picking up the brushes one by one and flipping them into the sink, where the paint oozed among the teacups. "Gatestead?"

"Gatestead?" said Dick. "Maybe."

"That family," said Grandma. "If you knew about that family what I know about it you wouldn't."

Bob thought it was time to join in. He was better at Grandma than Dick was. Bob picked up the last brush and stroked it tenderly. "If he did he would," he said.

"What are you butting in for?" said Grandma. "If I can't speak without being taken up at every other word I'll have you out of school and set to a trade at once. You know this place won't support you both when I'm gone."

"It supports us and Tot," said Bob, putting the brush in the sink with the others. It was the blue brush and it made a blue ring round the teapot.

"That old fool," said Grandma. "You know I only keep him on out of charity, nothing else. If he was given a day's work to do anywhere else he'd die."

"I'll get the bread out and the cups washed," said Bob.

Grandma pulled the cloth off her head. It had been held there with an elastic band. There was a red mark from it across her forehead. "Just wash one cup," she said. "I don't feel like cooking tonight. We'll go down to the village and have a pie." Before anyone could argue with her she was out of the kitchen and up the stairs, to change her clothes.

"Cooking," said Dick. "There's no cooking with bread and cheese and cups of tea."

25

"And there's none with pies down in the village," said Bob.

"You don't like going down there still?" said Dick. "You wash them and I'll dry them."

"She brought me up more," said Bob. "I understand her more."

"She was always trailing you off," said Dick.

Bob remembered being trailed off by Grandma. His mother had died when he was very young, and Grandma had been the only mother he knew. His father had been alive then, as well, and Grandma had been able to leave for a day or two at a time, taking Bob with her to Wakefield, where she had a sister, or to a friend's house in Morecambe, where the sea was. In those days going with Grandma was a colourful progress, with each journey an adventure into the unknown, destination uncertain, travel uncertain, money uncertain. Grandma had taken her watch to a pawnbroker before now to get the bus fare home.

Then her oddness had been a bright change from a dull world. Now her wild ways were an embarrassment, to be avoided if possible. Her ideas had grown more wayward and lasted less long. She had begun to paint the curtains, but Bob and Dick knew that she would not finish the first one. Already the flowers had begun to get larger and more ungainly as they came down the cloth.

Bob was looking at the flowers. "It's your fault," said Dick. "I think she's trying to keep up with things."

"I started her," said Bob. All he had done was describe how the girls in the form had been printing lengths of cloth with textile dyes, in the art room, using paper patterns they had made. Grandma had said that it sounded extremely fussy, and Bob had said that some of the results had been dismal with muddy purple or agonizing with green and red blotches. Grandma said that when she was a girl they had done fine sewing, and the gifted ones had done painting, and that the results had been neither dismal nor glaring, but artistic.

Two days later she was painting the curtains.

"Get the bread and cheese out, Bob," said Dick. "We might just get to stop in. If we go down to the village I'll never get to Gatestead."

Grandma came clattering down the stairs then, and looked sharply at the table. "Just the one plate," she said. "That's all he needs." She was wearing her shiny shoes with the high heels. She had on a yellow dress with a darn on the shoulder where it had got burnt. She had greenish eyelids, and she had brushed her hair out fluffy. It was bright blue at the moment, since her last rinse. "Now," she said, "I'll tidy up, and you two boys go and change. You can't be seen in the village like that."

"This is what I go to school in," said Bob.

"I've changed, you can," said Grandma. "Hurry up."

Outside there was a long warm dry twilight, with the white sky reflected in still waters. The fields full of growing grass were like silent tides disturbed and swelling, but scented like no sea, against the grey breakwaters of the walls. Staddle Hill to the north of Ravensgill rose up from the reticulated ocean like a fairy island, with the split tower on top like a temple.

"I wonder what pies have they tonight," said Grandma.

They had chicken pie and chips at the Heifer. Grandma would never go in the sensible cheerful place, the bar; but insisted on the chill parlour, shut away from everything that was going on. While they waited for the chips Grandma walked round the room as if it were the first room she had ever been in, though she had been in it hundreds of times. She checked on all the ornaments and re-examined each piece of furniture, and worked out what it was all probably worth. For the moment she was being an expert in these things.

"In my home we had a wealth of old furniture," she said.

"Where did you live?" said Bob, because he had never found out yet.

"It isn't there any more," said Grandma. "And it's very bad to get to. There were difficulties in the way." And then, as usual, she changed the subject.

The pies and chips came, and were eaten, and the strong tea of the Heifer drunk. After they had finished Dick said he ought to go up to Gatestead and see about the tractor.

"The tractor's all right," said Grandma. "I used it myself this morning."

"I was thinking of borrowing theirs for the cutting," said Dick. "Ours runs so hot."

"We don't borrow anything," said Grandma. "Then we don't lend anything. No one on my farm borrows anything. I never have and I never shall. When I'm gone you can do as you like; but not now. So you won't need to go to Gatestead, because you don't want to be calling on those people. They don't call on us, and we don't call on them."

"They're friends," said Dick. "I like to visit friends."

"Friends?" said Grandma. "They're no friends of mine. We've no friends here, nor anywhere. We look after ourselves. But if you're going there we'll all go. They won't keep us long if I'm there."

Grandma was getting excited, and she could not get excited

without becoming angry. Even happiness made her furious. Bob made one of his mistakes.

"It must be something in the vinegar," he said, picking up the vinegar sprinkler and sniffing it. Then the vinegar was leaking on to the tablecloth from the dropped sprinkler and Bob was rubbing his ear.

"They don't teach you decent Christian behaviour at school," Grandma was saying, folding her arms back together again after the thump she had given him. "It's time you were leaving that place and getting yourself something useful to do. You might just as well, because you're a form lower than you should be and you'll never come to anything in that line. You're not the one that deserves first-class treatment. I left school when I was thirteen, and if I'd learnt nothing else I'd learnt to respect my elders."

Dick picked up the vinegar and put it the right way up. He straightened the knife and fork on his plate, dusted some crumbs on to the floor, jogged his glasses up nearer his eyes, and stood up. "I'll be off, then," he said, and he got out of the door quick. Bob watched him go and sat still, wondering what would happen now, because defiance of Grandma led to trouble and pain.

Grandma watched the door closing behind Dick. Her nose sharpened and her chin came up. Her hand came on to the tablecloth, flat; then it contracted and took up a fold of the cloth. The vinegar fell over again. "I shall go home," she said. "I don't care what you two louts do."

"He has to go out sometimes," said Bob.

"Out? He's never in," said Grandma. "He comes into my house for meals, and that's all. And when we do meet, and I go out of my way to provide for him, what does he do? He walks out, after I've asked him not to. Some people will never be aware of decent behaviour, that's all."

Then she paid the bill, saying it was money wasted on the ungrateful, and they went out into the midsummer night.

The sun had set, but it was not far away, behind the hill to the north, Staddle Hill. Above the high rock shelves the dark sky grew thin, as if the night had been scrubbed clean of its shades. The edge of the hill was distinct and near.

Grandma had settled now into a hurt and sullen silence. The silence lasted until she and Bob were in the grass lane and walking up between the walls to Ravensgill. Then she became even more silent for a time, because she had taken a breath and held it, a sign that Bob knew. It meant she was coming out of her sulk.

"Do you know the stars?" she said. "Everyone should know the stars, but very few do."

The stars were not very much there to be known that night, because there was a high haze obscuring them. But they found The Plough, and Grandma discovered that the Pole Star was a long way out of position, and seemed to think it was the County Council's fault, Bob thought. He was not listening very hard to what she said, because he had got into a way of not heeding. Sometimes taking no notice was the only way to get other things done, like homework. Tonight he was wondering about Dick, and which way trouble for him would lie.

"And that's Orion," said Grandma, waving to an indefinite and almost starless region.

"And the nebula," said Bob.

"Not very distinct tonight, the nebula," said Grandma. "I'm

glad you learn something at school." When she said that Bob knew she had never heard of a nebula.

"Now what else is there?" said Grandma.

"I think I'll go to bed," said Bob, yawning at Orion and the nebula and the vagrant Pole Star.

"So shall I," said Grandma. "And when I go to bed I lock up, and if people aren't in they are out, and I shan't change my ways for anyone."

Bob went to bed, but he did not sleep. He waited for Grandma to come upstairs, but she did not come. He heard her tidy away the remains of Tot's supper, without washing the dishes. He saw the light from the kitchen window vanish from the wall outside, to be replaced by a fainter light. He did not hear the doors being locked.

He went to bed. He was woken by the noise of Dick getting into bed. Grandma was going to bed in the next room.

"She said she'd lock you out," said Bob. "I meant to stay awake and unlock the door. Did you get in?"

"She wouldn't do anything if she couldn't see what you did about it," said Dick. "She hadn't locked the door. She just sat up all pathetic with a candle, reading beside an empty grate, being neglected. I don't like it. I know it isn't really true, but she wouldn't do it if she didn't have to. I think everything I do hurts her feelings."

"Shake, friend," said Bob. "Anything anyone does upsets her. Was she always like that?"

"A bit," said Dick. "More since Father died, much more."

IV

GRANDMA WAS DOWN first in the cool summer morning. It was a Saturday, and Bob did not feel the pull of the school day hastening his own getting up. He listened to Grandma as she lit the kitchen fire. Lighting the fire was something he could have done for her himself, he thought. But he still lay there in bed even after Dick had got up and gone downstairs.

Outside, Dick and Tot were talking. Bob sat up and felt the cold air of the bedroom touch his shoulders. He pulled the window up and leaned out. Down in the yard Tot was about to leave to bring the cows down.

Bob shouted that he would go. Tot said that he was started on the way already.

"It's all right," said Bob, still leaning out of the window while he got one leg down into his trousers, and then tried the other. The leg he had dressed slipped into his shoe, and was ready. The other leg had difficulty. Bob found he had to undress and start again, or his trousers would be on backwards. Then he was ready, and tucking in his shirt and combing his hair with his hand, and leaping down the stairs three at a time.

"Are you getting some coals?" said Grandma.

"Going up for the cows," said Bob. "Shan't be long."

Then he was outside, taking a twist of woodsmoke with him from the new-laid fire. The ginger and white farm cat, sitting on the wall, was gold and ivory in the sunshine. Bob went from one side of it to the other, and even from the unilluminated side it sat in glory, with a rainbowed halo outlining it.

"Tatty moggy," said Bob, because he did not want to say Pretty Pussy. He thumped Tot on the back, and ran past him. Tot stopped walking and shook his head. He was an old man, and not quick enough any more to join in Bob's romps.

Bob went up the lane, running the edge of the shadow of the wall. In the sunshine the ground had dried, but in the shadow there were drops of dewy water, and damp shapes on stones that might have been the flowers of frost. In one place he thought he saw the living crystals of frost, but it might have been the dead crystals in the stone. When he bent to look there was nothing but dew.

The smell of grass came up from under his feet where the blades were crushed, and the smell of the earth itself where his shoe scarred the ground. From over the wall the meadow flowers threw their small shouts of scent, and beyond that again there was the faint sour smell of the moor itself.

Then, at the gate, there was the gross breathing of cows, oversweet, over-rich; and the brightness and overpowering flavour of their hides, and the pungency of fresh dung.

"Good morning, girls," said Bob, unlatching the gate and smelling the iron on his hands and the lichen on the gate.

The leading cow swung her head down and grazed up a little scalp of grass, and began to walk with her forked mechanical feet sliding on the earth. She stopped almost at once, lifted one of the hind feet, and scratched at her shoulder.

The following cows jostled each other, because they would not pass. Minnie came last. Bob gave her a slap on the rump as she went by. Then, instead of following them down, he went up the field they had been in, over the wall, and into the pasture beyond. This pasture was one of the allotments, and it was rough ground, cleared from the moor eighty years before. There was no heather on it now, but there was rank tussocky grass, a little gorse, and long shadings of reeds.

A little beck came from an outcropping rock, ran twenty feet, and went down into a pit, underground again. Where the water came out of the rock there was a spout, or fall. When Bob came out for the cows he often came the extra distance to this stretch of beck, and washed his face at this natural wash-place. It was much the same water as the tap at Ravensgill, but he would not be washing in competition with last night's cups and saucers, or drying on the damp threads of a greasy towel. Up here he dried on nothing but the air.

He let water run cold down his forearms, trickling off at his elbows, until the cold seemed more than his bones could bear. Then he swung his arms and sprayed the sky with the cold water, ran across the allotment to get away from the pinching that had run up into his shoulders.

He climbed a wall, and was on the moor again, in the enclosed part that was the gill itself. The water at the bottom of the slope ran steady. Higher up the hill he could hear it coming down the shelves of rock in the seven cascades to the pool at the bottom where the earth bank was that held the water back.

His stomach made a sheep-like noise at him. He found his hand going to his pocket to look for nuts, and stopped it, scratching himself instead, because he had to do something with the movement.

He turned to go back to the farm, along the edge of the gill. Now he could see that there was coal on the fire, by the colour and texture of the smoke. It came up straight, then a cross-movement of air caught it, and it drifted westwards. There was always a set of the wind up here, and in the still weather it set from the east.

There was no reason to hurry home, if breakfast was all he wanted, because there would be none until the milking was done. He went down because he might be able to help Grandma in some way. He always hoped that one day he would come in happy off the hill, and be allowed to stay happy. But always it happened that Grandma had some bitterness that made his joys of place and person shrink away again. Or if she had no bitterness to offer, she would in some way fill him with guilt, or shame.

This morning she managed to fill him with guilt. When he went in he found her struggling across the kitchen floor, hot and cheerful in a resigned way, with a sack of flour. She was bringing it from the room called the egg room to the dairy.

"You don't need to do that, Grandma," said Bob. "I'll soon get it across." He took the sack by the waist, pincered it with his elbows, and lifted it. Grandma opened the dairy door, and he dropped it into its place. It was all he could do to get it so far. If it had started life on a wagon he would have got it to shoulder height and carried it as far as he liked. But it was a cold lift from the floor.

"There's bread to make," said Grandma. "And you boys are so busy in the mornings." It seemed to Bob that she knew very well that he had only been walking about in the sunshine. He felt guilt about his treatment of her. The guilt crept in, and grew worse and worse, because he knew he did not always love or like or value this strange old woman, who was now clattering about in the hearth putting a bread bowl to warm. Then he was ashamed of his guilt and his dislike.

"I've got that moved," he said. "Is there anything else I can do?"

There were several other things to be done: more coal to be brought, the ashes to take out, the boiler to fill. The boiler was beside the fireplace, on the other side from the oven, and was filled with water from a smallish pail, because a bigger one could not get to the opening. The water went in and hissed against the warmed sides of the small square tank.

Along with the ashes he cleaned the flues, which was a pleasant job, if you were dirty already. There were hooked rakes that had to be put in through little flat doorways in the surround of the oven. The little doorways slid out of their places, and inside was the green breath of the smoke going on its way to the chimney. The hooked rake went in, and scraped the soot from the flat iron, and banged some away from the stone roof of the flue. The soot came out on to a shovel, and went out to the garden and was put near the onions.

He emptied the ashes from under the fire, and then scooped two or three bucketfuls from below the grating set in the hearth, and set the grating back in its place. It was the biggest help towards the cleaning of the fireplace to have the grating clear and not full. The darkness of the pit below outlined the holes in the grating, even though one was shining blacklead, and the other darkness of the same intensity. There was a difference in quality, with one shiny and uneven, and the other smooth and velvet.

Tot and Dick came in for breakfast. Tot, as usual, knocked on the door before coming in. He only came in for meals, and sometimes to sit by the fire if Grandma felt like inviting him. The rest of the time he lived in a room where cheese used to be matured, a room divided in two by the roof beam coming across at waist level. When he was young Tot used to hop over it, he said. Now he crawled under it if he had to go beyond it.

"It's rarely warm in here," said Tot.

"I've to make bread for all you people," said Grandma.

"There's no need to make it fresh for me, Lizzie," said Tot. "I've often told you."

"And I've told you often enough I can't make it stale," said Grandma. "If you're ready I've the bacon cooked."

"That's what we want," said Dick, settling himself at the table. Grandma looked at him.

"Do we?" she said. "We're welcome to our breakfast at least, Dick." She was talking about last night, when Dick had gone to Gatestead against her inclination and desire. As a sort of twisted revenge Grandma gave Dick the best piece of bacon, to make him sorry. If you got the best from Grandma it was because you had done something wrong. Dick said nothing more for some time.

After breakfast there was nothing to do. The next job on the farm was haymaking, and until the grass was ready to cut there was a tense space, where nothing else could well be started. Instead of going out and doing any of a dozen things that there was never time for in the rest of the year, they sat round the table and talked about past haytimes, when they had begun and when they had ended, and how the weather had been during them, and what the hay had been like, and how the tractor had broken down, because the tractor broke down every year. But a broken tractor was not the worst that could happen, because there was still the horse, black and called Dinah, to fetch and carry and draw the dasher or make windrows, or mow or pull the sledge.

Grandma gradually shifted them out of the room. For one thing she was heating the kitchen up with the fire, and for another she was making the bread. When she got to the stage of having the bread bowl spinning grindingly on the table among their arms and heads, as she kneaded the dough, they went out. It was nearly as warm outside as it had been inside.

"Ah?" said Tot. "If we could have it now it would be in the mewstead tomorrow, dry and fresh and never better. But it isn't there in the fields to cut yet, not rightly."

"Well, away then, Tot," said Dick, "we'll go up yon side and put up a gap in the moor wall. Are you coming, Bob?"

"I won't," said Bob. "I'll go up the gill a bit and maybe have a swim in the dub. I've to practise a bit."

Dick and Tot went off. Bob went in again and got his school bag. In the bottom of it were his wet towel and wet trunks. He put them under his arm, and went out again, and up the gill. He had more in mind than merely swimming in the dub, or pool behind the earth bank. He thought he might go to the top of the falls, and from there swim downstream, down the falls themselves, and after that down the gill, and perhaps out to the river in the bottom of the dale, two miles away. It would be nearly three miles altogether, by the map at school.

It was a thing he had often thought about: the longest swim

he could manage anywhere round here, unless he went to Vendale Water, and even there the circuit was only a mile. And it was not only the swim he wanted, but something else. Going down the gill would be like tobogganing, mostly a free ride. It would be an interesting swim, and a fast one, with the down-hill current.

He changed into his trunks by the earth dam. He thought he would try the falls at the top first, after looking carefully at them to see the dangers. He jumped into the dub, and swam across to the first fall, and looked for rocks below it.

Some time later he was high on the hill. The gill itself was not in sight. Above him was the confluence of three streams, none of them big enough to swim in. Beside him was the beck of Ravensgill, and below the flat plateau of the moor; and in the edge of the plateau, at the skyline, a little nick, where the beck took its first plunge. After that there were six more plunges among the rocks.

There was a little cool easterly wind ruffling the cotton grass. A hare started up at his feet, and he watched it curve away and become lost in the heather, its fur turned by the breeze. The same breeze was turning his fur, he thought, and getting below his skin. He dropped into the cool water and felt his shivering stop. He floated, still for a moment, and then felt the current take him gently. He helped the current with his feet, and watched the sky come closer ahead of him.

Then he was shooting forward into the sky, and suddenly the land shot up to where the sky had been, and he was going down with the water, down among the rocks. But he remembered what he had seen as he came up, though there was hardly time. He had it in mind to turn a little to the right, and he managed to do it, and he was under water, without the breath in his chest that he had hoped to take; but he was not striking rock.

Now the racing water took him in a swift-flowing channel towards the second fall, slithering him over the weedy surface of the rocks so that he felt the hard edges below. And he was down the second step of the journey. He stopped where he was for a moment, to check his position, holding on to a rock. He rehearsed the third fall, where he had to take the left branch or become grounded on a reef. He took the branch in time, and dropped his own length into a pothole that was worse than he had imagined, with the weight of water many times heavier than he had guessed. He pulled himself out of it, and sat on the rocks spitting and choking, until he felt cold again, and wanted to go on. Besides, he knew that the next three falls were nothing, just shallow steps in one rock plane. He managed them without difficulty.

The seventh, and last, fall was the tricky one. Or perhaps it was not tricky, but the worst to drop down. The last three had been one kind of rock, and there was no undercutting. But below the seventh fall there was the shale, and with the shale went undercutting, and with undercutting went breaking of the rock above. He was not worried about fresh rock falling. He worried about the height of the fall, and the rock already fallen. He had resolved not to look again before he dropped down; but now he was there he thought it would be idiotic not to look. He walked down to the edge and peered over.

The distance was no further than he could jump, and had jumped. There were three rocks to avoid, and all the rest was good water. Jumping is one thing, and committing yourself to the stream is another. But it was to be done, and he did it. He walked back again to where he had come out of the water, and let himself into it again.

He thought he was going down too fast, and tried to slow himself; but he had not time. The bottom dropped out of the stream suddenly, and he was falling, at all sorts of angles, and without being able to see where he was going. Then he felt water lifting his head, and began to put himself the right way up in it.

Then something struck the side of his head, and he lost his sense of balance, and did not know where he was. He felt he was in water and swimming, but he was under water and did not know which was up, because the pressure seemed to come on him from every side. He realized that he was swimming forwards, yet being dragged backwards, because now he felt the rocks below him, the bottom of the beck.

Then he was out of the pressure, and there was air to breathe; the current slowed, and he tried to lodge himself against something so that he could gather his wits, spit water, and count his limbs.

There was water in his ears, and he shook it out of one side. The other ear stayed full. In both of them there was the most appalling noise of water plunging and cascading. He shivered. And then he realized that he could hear and feel—water and rock and cold—but he could not see anything; and he knew that it was a bright sunny day and that he should be able to see, and that his eyes were open.

All the same, he could not see.

V

Dick and Tot walked down the lane together, deep in a conversation of silence. They were to leave the lane and turn off towards the stepping stones and ford over the water; but when they came to the turning-off place they saw the postman coming up the lane towards them, and waited for him.

"Poor old fellow he is," said Tot. "He makes a lot of that bank, he does."

"There's older folk, isn't there?" said Dick.

"There is," said Tot, knowing that Dick meant him. "And there's younger folk, and all. But some have more age on 'em, and that's a fact. Maybe some should retire, like, and make way."

Tot was talking of the postman, who was toiling slowly along, pushing his bicycle; but Dick wondered about something that was often in his mind, that he had never so far liked to ask.

"Does she pay you, Tot?" he asked. "Grandma."

"Your father used to pay me," said Tot. "Rich can pay poor, is what he said. Rich can pay poor. We called him Rich, for Richard, like you. Aye, I had money from him. Are you wanting it back?"

"Don't be a silly old beggar," said Dick. "We don't want it back. We should pay you more. We should pay you each week."

"I'm just an old fellow," said Tot. "I need nowt. I've my keep and my bed and my work; and if you pay me you'll own me. If I've need there's the workhouse, and it's not so bad there; and there's my brother in Vendale that's earning. Addling brass he is, pounds a week."

"I thought you weren't getting much," said Dick.

"She puts my 'baccy in the groceries," said Tot. "Like she would. That's all I need, summat in the groceries."

The postman came up and leaned his bicycle against the wall. He opened the bag and brought out three or four letters.

"Big load on today," he said. "There's even one for you, Thomas." Thomas is Tot said out full. Some people called him that.

"It'll be my brother," said Tot. "Is he right, do you think?" He took the envelope and looked at it, but without his glasses he could not see the writing on the envelope.

"Are you going on up?" said the postman. "Or shall I go up?"

"I'll have to go for my glasses," said Tot.

"I'll go up too," said Dick. "We're not that busy."

"That's best," said the postman. He put the brown mailbag on the handlebars, turned the bicycle round, and pushed himself off, freewheeling down the hill with the back spindle of the bicycle clicking as he went.

"It's not so oft I get a letter," said Tot, looking at the invisible inscription again. "I see a fine stamp, and that's all," he said.

"These are Grandma's," said Dick. "I don't get so many either."

Grandma was not pleased to see them again. On this hot day, with the fire burning large, she chose to be in the kitchen tidying the cupboard next to the stove. She was still in her mood of doing things to show Dick how she worked for him, to increase the force of the ingratitude he showed.

"I'll read them later, when I have time," she said. "And I don't want you men in my kitchen."

"I'm not wanting to be in," said Tot, who was still outside. He was on his way to his own room, to find his glasses. Dick put Grandma's letters on the table and went out to wait for Tot before setting off again for the wall that was to be repaired.

He could see Tot, up at the top of the outside steps, sitting on his bed in the little loft. He saw him lift his glasses down from some ledge among the stones of the wall, open the case, unfold the glasses, breathe on them and rub them on the bedcover and then introduce them to his face, where they were not very used to being. He saw him wrinkle his eyes and blink twice, and then look at the envelope, reading his name and address carefully. He excavated in his pocket for a knife, unlatched the blade, put the end under the flap of the envelope, and slid it along. Then, almost more slowly than Dick could bear to watch, he bedded the blade of the knife in its own groove, put the knife away, and picked up the envelope again. He had to inspect it carefully before finding where the opening was. He found it, pinched the sides together and slid them, so that an opening came, put in a large thumb and a large finger, and pulled out a sheet of paper.

He read it very slowly. The letter was only on one side, but he looked at the back of the page, and read the written side again. He folded the letter again, put it back in the envelope, went into another pocket, brought out a wallet, and put the letter in that. Then he unhitched his glasses one side at a time, pulling the wiry side-pieces from behind his ears, folded them,

44

and put the folded arrangement away. He got up from his bed, and came out of his room, closing the door behind him. He walked down the steps.

"Well then," he said. "It was to happen. What does she say to it?"

"What do you mean?" said Dick. "What?"

"She'll say summat," said Tot. "Maybe you don't know."

"No, I don't," said Dick. What he felt now was that something had happened that was to put things wrong; that the postman had brought letters with ill messages. 'Maybe you don't know,' Tot had said. Maybe Dick did not know; and maybe a worse thing, that though he could not imagine any particular thing, he could imagine that some catastrophe had come to Ravensgill.

"Is it bad?" he said.

"Summat and nowt," said Tot; but he said it gravely. "I'll ask her."

"Ask her what?" said Dick. "Tell me what you're talking about. What are you talking about, Tot?"

"It's not mine to say," said Tot. "But it'll be one thing off her mind."

Tot went to the kitchen door. It was closed, so that no draught would disturb the rising bread. He knocked on it, and walked in. Dick followed close behind.

Grandma had sat at the table to read her letters. One was a white one, and was a bill. The other was a page of blue writing on blue paper, the whole of one side and an inch of the top of the next page. Grandma had this letter in her hand, and she was staring at it. She was not reading it any more, and her eyes were not scanning. She was staring.

"I can see nowt," said Tot. "Did you hear, Lizzie?"

Grandma crumpled the edge of the paper in her hand. With the other hand she gathered up the other papers on the table. She stood up.

"I heard, Tot," she said. "Was it Wig?"

"It was to me," said Tot.

"And my cousin to me," said Grandma. "The brazzen-faced bitch, choosing to call me afresh after all these years. Her."

"It was good to hear," said Tot.

"Good to hear, oh hearken," said Grandma. "It makes no matter now; and nothing's changed that's done." She walked over to the fire and threw the two handfuls of paper on to the blaze. "I'm away to my bed," she said.

Dick was unable to know what to do. Speech was ready in him, but there was nothing to say. Help was willing in him, but he did not know what to help. But something had changed, he knew, and he knew that he had to join with something better than silence and stillness.

"Are you all right, Grandma?" he said, trembling, and like an idiot to himself.

Grandma looked at him with wax eyes. "Right enough, lad," she said. "Right enough." Then she was out of the room and going up the stairs.

"They're a pair," said Tot, as if he were talking about two famous queens. "Her and her cousin."

"I've never heard of her cousin," said Dick. "I haven't heard of anything. What is it?"

"Not mine to say," said Tot. "I'll be off and put up that gap. Will you stop or come with me?"

"I'll stop," said Dick. "You stop too, and do something in the yard. It doesn't matter about that gap."

"I'll find summat," said Tot. "And then."

Darkness pressed on Bob. Whether it came from his surroundings or from within he could not tell. There was nothing to be seen. He thought he might be under water, drowning; but his body was breathing, or it did until he noticed it, and then he was not sure.

He found that his head ached, and that there was a numbness all down one side, from shoulder to wrist and from hip to ankle. He found that the pain round the numbness was going, and being succeeded by a cold ache, not only in the side but all over.

The noise that had oppressed him began to clear. It did not grow less, but it sorted itself out. Water ran from the ear that had stayed blocked. Then he was able to tell one noise from another. All the noises were water noises, but some were near by and some were further off, and some of the noise was not fresh source-noise but echo and reverberation.

He thought that if he sat still he would be able to see again, find out what bank of the beck he was on, and make his way down to the farm. He thought too that even if he did not recover vision, that he would still, in a little while, be able to pick his way along the bank.

The sun had stopped shining. There was no warmth coming on to him at all. There was not any warmth left in the ground, either, as there would be if clouds had come on the sun, or if night had come. There is always heat left to be thrown out of walls and earth and rock. There was nothing now.

Bob moved. He had been sitting collapsed among rocks and stones, and his own weight had pressed him on to them. When he eased his limbs from their positions his skin shouted at him, and water ran icy over new areas. He stood up.

He had expected the darkness over him to be sky, distant and untouchable. It was not. It was rock. His head hit it, and he almost went down again. A steadying hand touched rock beside him, and held him firm.

Now he was frightened. When he thought he was blind he had been terrified, but blindness does not mean death. It is not a symptom of the end of life. The world is still with you in blindness; and all you have to do is feel for it in other ways than with your eyes. But the rock over his head, that had struck him, was a symptom of death, because it meant that he was underground. It was not blindness, it was not eclipse of eyesight, it was darkness that left him with no view of the world; and the darkness was the darkness of the underground world. It meant he had no surroundings he could know. His place was a strange one to him, and he had no way of knowing how to get out, no chance of being met by anyone else and being led home. He was alone, in some watercourse, under the hill.

But if he knew that death was looking at him he knew as well that life was inside him. And that if there was no one else to help, he had to help himself. He thought that if he had come in with the water that pounded against his feet, then he had come downstream with it. He crooked one elbow round his head to protect it from rock, and bent down to feel the water. He felt the tug and tow of it, and knew how it ran. He knelt in it and began to walk upstream.

He walked, on his knees, through a slippery pool, and came to the bottom of a waterfall. It was three feet high, and he climbed up it. He was now on a gentle rising slope, smooth and rock-free, and perhaps not natural. He crawled up it, thigh deep and elbow deep in a smooth skin of water, running quietly near by, but roaring further away.

He knew where the water lay after a little while. It was as if his skin grew more sensitive to the feel. He thought he might be getting dry, over the part of him that was not in the water. The sense of knowing by some uncanny means where the water was grew stronger. It was no uncanny thing. There was light on the water, and his eyes were seeing it.

There was double hope in him now, for not being blind, and for finding a way out of the earth.

The slope went on gently. The sides of the place he was in began to close in. He could see water shining on them as they came closer. At last he saw the shape of the tunnel he was in, cut square in the rock, lined level probably with concrete, and going up to a greenish square ahead.

The greenish square was the way out. It was about four feet each way, and water was coming in for half the height, with a strong and steady rush. The pull of it dragged Bob down under itself. If he had not had rough rock in the wall to hold to he would have been pulled back down the slope. As the water went down the slope it spread and shallowed. Beyond the slope there was noise coming back up, where the rock began again, where Bob had found himself at first.

Now he saw a stone lintel, and beyond the lintel the far shore of the dub behind the earth dam, and the glittering water of the pool itself, and the foot of the fall, where water broke white on fallen rock.

He did not get out quickly. When he was used to seeing the bright outside he could not see the gloom inside. He tried to push his way through the opening where the water was coming. He could not get through. His shoulders were too numb to tell him what was wrong. They only came up against resistance. Bob looked with his eyes and mind, and discovered three bars across the opening, thick bars that left less than a foot to squeeze through. He could not align himself to get his body between any pair of them, with the water pulling at him, and the numbness of cold thickening his responses. He pushed vainly, and the bars stayed where they were.

He found himself shouting. He heard the noise of it, and wondered where it came from. It was his own throat. He gave up trying to get through the spaces between the bars, and let himself sink down into the water, giving up his own rescue. He was spiting fate, giving himself up to it before it could do as it wanted, because fate takes you against your will. He thought he would swing with fate's direction, and perhaps be released out of pity.

He was. He let himself down into the water, still clinging to the bars. And below water-level the bars had rusted and rotted away. There was a wide gap, not very deep, but well fitted for a swimming body. Bob swam and struggled through the gap, feeling the ends of the bars above and below holding his skin and snagging his bones. But he got through, and a moment later he was standing in the sunlight, in the dub, blinking at the new world and wondering why there was salt in his mouth from his own tears.

VI

"IT's VERY GRATEFUL, sitting in the sun," said Tot. He was hunkered down on the stump used for chopping wood. His knife was in his hand again, not opening letters this time, but slicing tobacco into his palm.

He and Dick had found there was nothing worth starting in the yard before dinner. There was really nothing worth starting before haytime. They had looked at the felt on the henhouse roof, and decided that to repair it would be too much outlay of work, and that it could wait until cooler days. "You don't want to be tewing on with that felt on a day like this," said Tot. "Hoisting and hauling."

Dick was sitting on the grindstone, with one foot on the handle. He could rock himself gently from side to side and make the axle squeak if he wanted. Tot said it would put an edge on him if he tried it.

There was no sound from the house. There was a little feminine gossip from the hens, two or three of which had got up and looked at the roof of their hut, as if they knew what had nearly been in Dick's mind. In the sheaf of sycamore trees at the end of the yard the insects held mart and bazaar. Away down the gill the water gently clattered. Round about the still sky full clouds formed and hung.

Tot's match sang out and burnt with invisible flame. Blue smoke came from the bowl of his pipe, and a mistier blue from his mouth. The match went on the ground, and curled and died with a little scratching sound.

"I'll go in a minute," said Dick. "There might be summat."

"She's right, you know," said Tot.

Dick got off the grindstone and walked across to the house. He went into the kitchen, and stood there. He smelt the bread rising in the hearth, and the heat of the oven-metal. He heard the water boil in the tank beside the fire. The kitchen was very hot.

Upstairs there was a sound. He heard Grandma's bed creak, and her feet on the cotton rug, and then on the lino, and then again on the bare boards at the edge of the room. He heard her open the wardrobe door, and move something about, making a banging that he could not name, though he had heard it before.

She walked again, and this time opened the bedroom door. He heard the latch rise and fall. Grandma began to come down the stairs, slowly. Something she was carrying banged against the wall. Then she was down, and would be beside the front door, which was hardly ever opened. Dick waited for her to come into the kitchen.

She did not come. She paused at the bottom of the stairs, and then went up again, quicker than she had come down. In her bedroom she paced about again, and once more came the noise Dick could not place.

Once more she stepped downstairs, once more paused in the little hall of the house, and once more went upstairs again, closed the bedroom door behind her, and continued the activity.

Dick went out of the kitchen, into the room beyond, and opened the door beyond that, leading to the front door and the stairs. The house was cooler here, and never was warm. The sun shone full on the front door, and he could see its light through a crack in one of the panels. Sunshine was lifting an oily smell from the ringed pattern of the lino on the stairs. There was nothing in the hall. He stepped across the empty space, and looked in the parlour beyond. He felt like a spy as he did.

In the parlour, beside the black prickly hair sofa with the red wood framing, stood two suitcases. Sunshine was on them too, and in the sunshine were the agitated motes of dust stirred by Grandma when she had brought the cases down and set them there.

The bedroom latch went click again. Dick stepped back across the hall, into the front room, and closed the door. He went back into the kitchen, and listened to Grandma as she came down again as she had done before. And again she went up.

In the kitchen the smell of bread rising was insistent. Dick looked in the hearth, and saw that the dough had come up over the bowl and hung over the side, and was resting a white buttock on the new-fallen ashes. He lifted a corner of the cloth, and found that it had stuck slightly to the top of the dough. He gave it a little tug, and that upset the texture and balance of what was in the bowl. There was a sigh and a settling, and the puffy top sank down again as if it had breathed out. Dick tiptoed out of the kitchen. He was prepared to be caught spying on Grandma, but he was not ready to be blamed for spoiling the bread.

He came back and sat down on the grindstone again, without being able to make himself comfortable. He perched and twisted, and then came down, and sat on the ground.

"She's packing," he said, hoping for a reaction and useful comment from Tot.

Tot said nothing for several breaths, each one counted with smoke. "Aye," he said. "Well, that leaves thee and me and Bob, doesn't it?"

"Is she going?" said Dick. "Where would she go, why would she go?"

"She might say," said Tot. "But it's not mine to tell. I'm stopping on the right side and saying nowt. You ask her."

"But there must be a reason," said Dick. "That letter."

"There will be a reason," said Tot. "There was a reason. But there was bound to be a time when it was all over, and maybe this is it. Maybe she's no need to stop here any longer now."

Now that he was out in the world Bob began to wonder who he was and what he was doing. For some time he had considered only his flesh and mind and blood, and how they could be preserved. Now that he had brought them to a place he knew was safety he thought of other things. First he remembered being in the water for a long time, in sunshine before going into darkness. For a minute or two, standing shivering in the sun, it seemed that he might have lived all his life in the water. But then, and as if he had drawn it himself, he saw his own walk up the gill, and behind it his breakfast and going to bed last night: his life grew out from the place he was in now, and as it grew it filled his mind, so that he was placed at last.

For a while, though, he stood the other way round in time, seeing the past roll itself out ahead of him, as if he saw it with his eyes; and the future was out of sight, but only because it was physically behind his back.

He knew where he was now, in place and time. He walked out of that place and time, to the edge of the dub, and climbed the earth bank, and sat on the grass near his clothes. The towel, laid damp there, had dried in the sun, dried stiff. He put it over his shoulders, and it was like laying a rough stick there, because of the tenderness. He could not see his back; but he could see his arms and legs and his chest. He saw that he was bleeding, bruised, and scratched. He was a farmer, and he naturally counted his sheep: eighteen rising bruises and thirty-three bleeding wounds visible "from where I'm sitting" he said to himself, because externality was coming back in ripples.

The towel softened. He used it to dab water from himself; and with the water came a little blood, because no scratch was deep. He looked, he thought, as if he had been scrubbed for a moment with rough sandpaper with one grain of sand every six inches.

The sun warmed him. He heard his breathing. It was still a gulping, panic breathing; how the little boys breathed when they were first put into the swimming pool by the next form up. Bob caught at the edge of his breathing cycle when it was at the top of a stroke and still. His chest tried to empty itself, but he held it back, though it was like a strange other person's chest. Then he breathed out slowly, and in slowly, and felt his muscles lose their emergency grip.

He was dry now. There were no shivering stretches of skin

where evaporation caused local chills. He put the towel on his head, but had not the strength to move it actively. He leaned back in the grass, and it stabbed him as he settled. He lay there and let the sun wash him. He pulled a flap of towel over his eyes to keep the brilliant circumstantial orange light from his retina. He felt the familiar finger and thumb of sleep pinching and pushing the bridge of his nose and the inner edges of his eye-sockets. Then the sound of the water went away from him, and his hands left him, and he slept.

There was a dream. In it he was running across the school playground. It was the playing field of his present school, in fact, but he knew it was the playground of his primary school to a greater extent. He was running, and the rest of the school, particularly the top class of the primary school, was laughing at him for losing his clothes gradually, and he was becoming more and more alarmed himself about it, because it signalled more meaning than he could comprehend. In the loud shouting of the world of school he looked down at his running legs, and saw on one ankle his trousers swinging, but not quite his own trousers, but red pants like Marilyn Shepherd's, and he was very ashamed because that proved he was a girl, and the shouting grew louder, and went away as he woke up, though not completely away. He sat up, and a thousand mouths of pain on his back and sides grimaced.

He was alone with the beck and the sun. There was no crowd about him, and no calling; but he felt that they had been not far off, as if they might leap out from the other side of a rock or come up from the water. But he forgot about them in a moment, because he worried still about Marilyn Shepherd's red pants, and why they should be round his ankle. He found what the dream meant almost at once. The dream had tried to say something about red bathing trunks, without being able to find the right picture for them. It had looked for something red not quite trousers, and come up with the nearest thing; and it had been telling him what he had not noticed: that he had gone into the water in his trunks, and come out without them. He had lost them somewhere under the earth. There was a label on them to recognise them by, numbered 172, because they were school equipment. They should not have been brought home at all, but they often were. He pulled on his shirt, then his own pants, which were the greyish white that Grandma's washing achieved. He pulled on his socks, and then his trousers, dipped his feet into his shoes, and stood up.

He had an ache in the back of his head that he thought would overbalance him. He adjusted its burden, and began to walk down the gill, picking his way over the tussocks of grass. He felt safe and well now, with a locatable pain in his head, a skin of cuts and bruises, and feet that could walk and go and eyes that could see.

He came in sight of the farm, where it rested on the side of the hill, in its own daysleep, having grown its own shell against time. He thought of it as a burrow in eternity, where animals, people, lived secretly.

There was a piece of scorched blue paper lying on the grass of the hillside. There was blue writing on it, on one side only. Bob picked it up, put it in his shadow, and read it.

'has told me a danger is past and the watcher has died. I hear that you have yet nothing and hardly have hoped it, but I have plenty and will share if you do not expect to be forgiven I should like to see you before I die still it was murder the jury said and you let him go. I will give to you in charity cousin, it is what the book says not my heart I cannot forgive. But you are still my own sweet girl 1 loved and played with then and I am glad danger is gone from you, I do not know what I think, if you'

There the writing ended. Bob read it through twice, and wondered if it could be part of life at all. Then thinking made his head ache even more. He walked on with the letter, putting the damp towel at the back of his neck to ease the aching.

He came into the yard, in the welcome shadow of the buildings. The yard was empty, and the kitchen door was open. He saw Dick and Tot inside, and Grandma by the kitchen range.

Dick had asked Tot what reason there could be for Grandma to go away. It was a thing she had not done for years. Once she had taken Bob away two or three times a summer; but now she had hardly been further than the village for five years, ever since Dick's father had died. Tot shook his head, and would not say anything.

Then Grandma herself had come out of the kitchen door, dressed in a way that Dick had hardly ever seen: a long black coat, with a black dress under, a black straw hat, dark stockings, and the gingery skin of an animal complete with its head and eyes hung round her neck.

"If you'll come in I'll give you your dinners," she said.

So they had gone in and sat at the table, while Grandma laid the table under their elbows, with old bread and cold bacon. She had taken a knife to the new dough and sliced away what had touched the floor, leaving a bubbled fringe hanging upwards. What had hung down was kneaded into the bowl again.

"You'll have to take that out when its time comes," she said. "I think I might go home. You'll have Tot, I don't want him following me again, silly old fellow."

Tot listened and said nothing. Grandma held out the kettle to him and he filled it at the tap. "That would have made me laugh, once-over," he said.

"And me," said Grandma, severely, taking the kettle back from him. "And give up your nonsense."

She thrust the kettle into the fire. She asked where Bob was, but they did not know. She said he had better be here soon, or she would not be there.

Then Bob came walking slowly in. As he came Dick saw that in his hand there was the letter that had upset Grandma, that she had thrown in the fire, and which the fire had blown up through the chimney, he now understood, and left where Bob would find it. Dick jumped up from the table, and went out of the door as Bob came in through it, knocking Bob down on to his back, and snatching the paper. He crumpled it up, stepped to the fire, and pushed it under the kettle, and the flame of it curled up the side of the kettle and left a dark moss of soot on the handle.

Bob got up, came into the kitchen, and sat down. He gazed at Dick. Dick shook his head and touched his lips, and nodded at Grandma's back. She was putting tea in the pot. Bob tried to join together the matter in the letter and Grandma. Something came unstuck somewhere. Even Grandma was wrong, because her clothes were wrong. Grandma did not dress like that, and she never had.

He looked at his plate. It was empty and innocent. Then Dick cut the bacon, and laid a slice on Bob's plate. Bob looked at it without thinking of hunger, or any other thing. He put out his hands and picked up knife and fork, cut the cold bacon, and put a piece in his mouth and chewed it.

Grandma put the teapot on the table, setting it down heavily, and making the table tremble. Bob felt the trembling; but it would not stop, but continued. The table rattled, and his limbs rattled, and in along the edges of the rattling the world turned negative, black where white had been, and white invisibility where dark had been; and then he floated away backwards into a swoon, hearing his knife and fork and plate fall with him to the ground.

When he woke up he was being sick on the floor, time after time, with Grandma holding him. He was crying too. The body that was vomiting was in the kitchen, lying on the rug; but the great swollen throbbing head was filling the whole of the sitting-room, and the legs, he knew, were out in the yard.

There was more darkness in a while; and after that Dick was taking him upstairs, which was impossible because Dick would never have been able to walk through the head that filled the sitting room, and the head would be too big, as well, to come up the stairs.

Then there was bed, and light and dark and light and dark, and it was Monday morning again, and Dick getting up to milk.

"Stop there," said Dick. "I'll tell Grandma you've woken."

But when Grandma came in Bob was asleep again.

"He's right enough now," said Grandma. "But I doubt you'll none of you ever be ready to be left." And it seemed that she was not going, because over the week-end she had shed her black clothes, and resumed her Gypsy Queen bright tatters, and taken her cases upstairs.

Bob slept.

VII

IT WAS SATURDAY. Judith was helping Wig to clear some old straw from the mewstead, against the time when the fresh hay would be brought in.

"We'll fire it," said Wig. "It's no use for owt." Judith wanted to go for matches at once, but Wig said he wasn't going to have little scratty fires all over the spot. There'd be more rubbish, he said, and it could all go into one heap, and no hurry to fire it.

"Don't fire it when I'm at school, that's all," said Judith. "Then I can get it into an essay."

Wig sat on the outside steps of the building, because he had finished pitching straw over the edge, and said it was a long time since he had heard that word. "Maybe fifty years," he said. "Where's t'mine?"

"Your what?" said Judith.

"The shaft, where they're digging," said Wig. "If there's an essay there must be some ore, and if there's ore there must be a mine. But they've all stopped: there's no lead left in the hills; they got it all out."

"It's a different kind of essay," said Judith. "We've to write things down, like a story where nothing happens except descriptions. Like 'My Day at the Seaside'."

"That's a composition," said Wig. "We'd to do them at school, I remember. But I'd left school when I was your age, and I was out working, same as I am now."

"You're sitting on the steps in the sun," said Judith.

"Saturday afternoon," said Wig. "We don't work so hard of a Saturday these days. I worked for your grandmother's father, old Mr Dinsdale, brother to the one there was the trouble about with Lizzie, that would be some sort of cousin to you if she was alive. Well, she is alive, but that's all. She's not heard of."

"That's the one they won't tell me about," said Judith. "But you will, won't you?"

"If they won't, I'd best not," said Wig. "It's nowt to do with me. I'm just a labouring man, and it never concerned me. My brother might tell you; but I'd better not."

"What about the brother to the old Mr Dinsdale that was my great-grandfather?" said Judith. She was meaning to be calm now, though what she felt was impatience that something was not at once explained to her. She wanted to shake Wig when he looked at her calmly and said "He's dead, you know."

"I know he's dead," said Judith. "They all are, aren't they?"

"Aye," said Wig. "That was the trouble."

"The policeman," said Judith. "The one that was after Lizzie. Did she kill him?"

Wig looked at the building opposite for a while before he spoke. "First," he said, "don't talk so lightly, as if life and death came to nowt in your mind. We should die at the appointed time, which the Lord gives, not by the hand of man. And next, of course Lizzie had nowt to do with it: she was here all the time, and it happened way over, in another place."

"I know," said Judith. "It was Ravensgill."

"It was," said Wig. "I don't know how you came to it, but it was. So maybe you know plenty."

"I don't even know where Ravensgill is," said Judith.

"I was never there in my life," said Wig. "But I've a brother there, that's all. It's seven or eight miles off by road, but not so far over the top, but you can't get that way over Staddle Moss and Huker Mire. They're bad places; and that's where . . . Well, never mind about that."

"You have to tell me," said Judith. "Where what? Where who? How did he die, what did the policeman do?"

"He did nowt," said Wig. "Because Lizzie hadn't done owt either."

"I want to know why," said Judith.

"Maybe it was a Saturday afternoon," said Wig; and he let himself drop off the step he was sitting on, down to the ground, and walked off towards his cottage and garden, where he would never let anyone come.

Judith stuck the hayfork in the heap of straw and went to see what Mick was doing. She found the two little ones first, with a dolls' wash-day on the lawn in front of the house. There was a camp going on at the same time, with a counterpane over a clothes horse on its side. Judith had to go in, crawling, to see the arrangements inside this tent, kinking her knees against the bars on the ground. There was nothing in the tent at all, but a bowl of suds; but she had the beds and shelves and the cooking stove and the bathroom and the gear-box (the little ones often had gear-boxes in their tents and houses) explained to her. She approved of it all, and went on to find Mick.

He had found there was nothing to do for an hour or so, until dinner time. To Wig any time after about eleven in the morning was afternoon. He liked to have his dinner then, but now he had to wait until one o'clock, or even later, because times had changed with the coming of electricity. Days were longer now all the year round. So while Wig was taking his afternoon off Mick was taking part of the morning off.

"I'll teach you to swim," he said.

"I nearly know," said Judith, making swimming movements with her arms. "Anyway, it's against the law, or something."

"Shaff," said Mick, meaning Nonsense. "It's empty." He was talking about the reservoir, where swimming, fishing, boating, and anything interesting were all forbidden by the Water Board. But the people of New Scar House had used it as a swimming place for years. Judith knew Daddy had often dropped himself into it when he was younger, and his father before him.

"I'll just watch you," she said to Mick. "I won't come in myself."

"O.K., drip," said Mick. "Do you know Bob White? Is he in your form?"

"Did he really win you?" said Judith. "They said he did."

"He did, really," said Mick. "Not by much, but he did."

"Will he be in the inter-schools sports?" said Judith.

"Not if I can beat him in the next set of finals," said Mick. "And I want to, so don't you start about letting the best one win, and not being a bad sportsman and everything, because I want to win, and if I do I'll be the best one winning, and he'll have to think about being the sporting loser. So shut up and come on down to the rezzy."

"I'm not sympathetic," said Judith. "I don't agree at all with your pride and prejudice and sense and sensibility and your war and peace."

"What are you raving about?" said Mick.

"I don't see why you have to be better all the time, and have to push past everyone like that," said Judith. "All you boys do the same, you can't join together and find out who's best at something and then help them to do it best. You're doing it for the school, not for yourself. If Bob White can swim faster than you why not go and help him, instead of trying to beat him?"

"Perhaps it's because it's Bob White," said Mick. "I have to beat him. One reason is that he's about a year younger."

"Age hasn't got anything to do with it," said Judith. They were walking down the lane towards the reservoir now, leaving a silvery dust in the air because the track had a silvery sand on it. The yellow-flowered weed in the verge of the roadway has leaves that are silver on one side: here they were silver on both sides; and the flowers made the borders parcel-gilt. Above them, and against the field walls, the wild roses hung like silver tarnished, and the same dust, instead of lightening them, darkened them.

Mick had had to think about the value of age. "It doesn't matter much about age," he admitted.

"Of course not," said Judith. "They don't make the oldest person Queen, do they?"

"Another thing," said Mick. "When I leave next month I won't be able to compete again, will I? But he can compete again next year and the year after, and perhaps after that, if he goes on into the sixth form."

"You're thinking about yourself," said Judith. "You should think about the school."

"And there's another reason," said Mick. "It's because he's Bob White; but you don't know anything about that."

"What's wrong with that?" said Judith. "That just sounds like hate and hateability. What's he done to you, except swim faster?"

"I won't tell you," said Mick. "Are you coming down to the edge of the water, or are you going to watch from the top?"

"I want to know what you won't tell me," said Judith. "All day people haven't been telling me things. First Wig wouldn't tell me about..."

"Tell you about what?" said Mick.

But Judith had remembered the letter posted the night before, addressed to Mrs White, at Ravensgill; so that the name Bob White, and the place Ravensgill came together. "Oh," she said. "I know all sorts of things, I didn't realize."

"I'm not going to talk any more," said Mick. "There is such a thing as pride."

Judith went down with him to the edge of the water. The level was low, and they had to pick their way over loose-lying stones, cracked and crazed in appearance because of the mud that had dried on them. There were successive tide marks where the water had risen again and retreated once more, and there were thickets of white wood like antlers water-washed and fronded with dry weed. Judith pulled at some of the smaller pieces and hauled them higher up the bank, above the stone layer to the sand. Mick changed behind some living bushes, and picked his way to the water.

"Watch my feet," he said.

"Wash them yourself," said Judith; and he shouted the instruction again. His voice was swallowed by the water, both in the surface never still, and by the slow crackle of wavelets along the rocky edge. A moment after Mick's shout there came back a split and shattered echo from the far side, where the hill rose out of the reservoir. Along the hill, rising from the water with it, was a construction of arches, as if someone had built half a cathedral there, a long nave buttressed and bleak with filled stone windows. It was some sort of retaining wall to hold a loose slope. Down two of the windows ran water, summer and winter, a steady flow. At the foot of one of the arches was the outlet of a bigger watercourse, barred, and flowing down in a channel from wall to wall. The whole of the opening showed now, but when the reservoir was full only the top two or three feet opened into the hill.

So Mick swam, and Judith idly watched his feet, not knowing what she was looking for. Mick turned and swam back, and came out of the water. "Mr Lankester says my legs are untidy," he said. "That's what I'm practising."

During the next week Bob White was not at school. Mick was chosen to go forward to the next heats to represent the school. Mr Lankester helped him with his legs, and told him his breathing was not too bad.

He had a fright, though, the next Friday evening. He had been milking with Wig, and then come in to steal strawberries from the jam-making. It was Judith's jam, and she and Gran were doing it all. The jam was for the Parent-Teacher Association stall, and the open evening next week. Mother said she would rather give a pound, money, than slave away making things, because if people wanted to raise money they always got more by asking for it honestly. But Gran and Judith thought they ought to get something for the money, and Judith thought jam, and argued Gran into helping with it. So they spent almost exactly a pound on fruit and sugar, and began to cook it.

"Don't touch them, they're weighed," said Gran to Mick; but he could not keep his hands off one strawberry rolled in the ready sugar. It was preserving sugar, and crunched between his teeth.

They were in the kitchen. Mother was upstairs getting the little ones to bed. Someone came to the door and stood there, looking in, and raising a hand to tap on the glass.

"Good evening," said Gran. She was nicely ahead of herself now, and not wanting to be disturbed, writing labels for the jars, saying 'Early Strawberry, made at New Scar House', followed by the date.

"From the Water Board," said the man.

"I'll get Daddy," said Judith; and she went for him out of the shippon.

"They'll have been testing the supply," said Daddy. He swilled his hands and dried them, and came to the kitchen door.

"Now then," said Daddy. "You want to come when there's been a bit of rain, and then you'll see our water at its foulest."

"Mr Chapman?" said the man. "I'm not your local board. I'm from Claro and Craven, about the reservoir."

"Oh, yes," said Daddy. The man brought something out of his pocket. It was a plastic bag, with something in it.

"What is it?" said Daddy. "Dead cat?" The man handed it to him. Inside there was a pair of red swimming trunks.

"Do these belong here?" said the man, looking at Mick. Mick crunched sugar, and put out his hand for them.

69

"Not mine," he said. "Mine are blue. But these are school ones, because there's the label with G.C. on, and the number."

"G.C.?" said the man.

"Garebrough Comprehensive," said Mick.

"Does the school lend them out?" said the man.

"It lends them in," said Mick. "We can't bring them home."

"You mean you shouldn't?" said the man. "Do you mind if I ask him a few questions?"

"Carry on," said Daddy. "He's got his own trunks here."

Mick produced his own, and said again that he had never brought any back from school.

"We were suspicious, you know," said the man. "Boys will be boys, you know, and there's no swimming in the reservoir, and these were found at the edge of it. So I just wondered, and I hope you don't mind. I'll take them down to the school and give them back." Then he and Daddy wandered off into the lane, talking about water supplies.

"I think I need another strawberry," said Mick. "I thought they must be mine, even if they were red. Because they were wanting to cop somebody for swimming, and it ought to be me. I expect they will."

"Leave those strawbugs alone," said Judith, clouting him with the wooden spoon.

Judith saw the next part of the story of the trunks; but Mick did not. On Tuesday, during a History lesson, the form room door opened, and the headmaster came in, and asked for a minute. "White?" he said. Bob looked up. "Have you a pair of swimming trunks belonging to the school?"

Bob said yes, he had, because he hadn't any of his own. Then he was asked to produce them if he could. Then the headmaster threw them to him, and he caught them.

"I'm not going to tell the whole school," said the headmaster, "because that would give the youngest ones ideas. But those trunks were found in the Claro and Craven Water Board's reservoir at the head of the dale—where you live, Judith Chapman—and they've asked me to remind you that swimming is not permitted. All I can say is that if you must go swimming in forbidden waters, please don't use school property, which shouldn't have been taken home in any case, White. But I can't think what you were doing right up there, White. It's about as far from where you live as anywhere is."

The headmaster went out, and the bell rang for the end of the lesson.

"I've never been there," said Bob. "Nowhere near. And I was in bed all last week, right from Saturday morning, and I can't think how they got anywhere, and I didn't drop them on the way home, because I can remember them the next morning in my school bag. But I was in bed all the time after."

Judith listened to what he said. For a moment he reminded her of her grandmother trying to remember a name or where she had put something half an hour before.

"I nearly knew," said Bob. "I've never been near your reservoir, have I, Judith?"

"I don't think so," said Judith. "But . . . Well, never mind."

VIII

BOB HAD BEEN in bed until Friday, and then he had to get up.
For several days he had lain under the weight of his aching
head, opening his eyes to watch moving shadows on the ceiling,
coming in over the curtains. The room had been hot, and he
had smelt his own sweat like a decay around him.

When his head had stopped aching and he was able to reckon
it was down to its own size, he found that his body was the
home of the aching. All his skin had dried and become tender,
and the flesh below it tensed itself in bruises and did not like to
be moved.

He lay there, slow in mind and body, watching Dick get up
in the morning, waiting for Grandma to come to him and bring
him drinks and offer him thin bread or eggs.

One day she asked him how he had come to have all the
bruises and breaks and scratchings on him. Bob told her he
did not know, because he had no idea. Until then he had
thought that his pain was due to his sickness, and his disease
had brought him to his sick-bed.

Grandma sat on the bed, next to him, and stroked back his
hair from his eyes. Her cool hands ran over his skin like water,
and her gold ring touched him like ice. "I never saw anyone so

bruised," she said. "Except once. Yes, once. Now, Bobby, tell me, what did you do on Saturday morning?"

"I walked up to the gill, right to the top," said Bob. "And then I walked right down again, and I came in, and Dick managed to walk into me and knock me down. Then I had my dinner and I had this bad headache. That's all."

"You collapsed with great drama at the table," said Grandma, "just when I was having to go away for a day or two on urgent business. But never mind about that."

Bob took Grandma's hand and squeezed the cold frail bones together. He knew that the urgent business was some sort of invention, though there was something true about it. Grandma was able to take parts of things and add them up to something very like truth but different from everything it had risen from. That was her silliness, because she did not know that she was more than Grandma to him: she was like his mother. But every time she decorated reality with tempting colour, so that he would see how she strove for him, she mismanaged. She did not know that he would love her as a mother and a grandmother without any help.

There was truth in what she had said about going away. He could remember that she had been dressed in the clothes that long ago had meant a sudden trip somewhere. The clothes had been out of sight so long that they were strange as well as familiar.

"You were going to Wakefield," he said. "To your cousin."

"Another cousin, that I haven't seen for many years," said Grandma. "She's older than me, and possibly dying; and I have expectations there, and rights as well. But it can wait."

"Where?" said Bob. "Far away, like Wakefield?"

"Not far away," said Grandma.

Bob knew that something must have happened to him between leaving the house and coming back to it. He could remember being at the head of the gill, on the plateau of the moor. He could remember walking along the side of the gill, coming towards home again, reading a blue paper, and he was clear in his mind that he had come back to Ravensgill with the blue paper in his hand, and made an instant connection between the paper and Grandma, who was dressed in her going-away clothes. Dick had made the connection clearer by jumping on him and taking the paper away, as if he recognised it and knew what it said. Bob remembered reading the paper, but nothing in it would come to mind.

By Friday Grandma's attentions had ceased. She had tired of playing nurses, he thought. She was busy again playing Grannies, and being too old to walk up the stairs with a tray. Bob had to come down now if he wanted anything.

On Saturday he got up with Dick, and led the cows down, and walked not very quickly up to the water-source where he washed his face. The cows went down by themselves, and he walked down the gill. There was the place where the blue paper had been; but the root of ling where it had lain was empty of recall: nothing came to his mind again. He was a week late with himself.

He went down to breakfast. After breakfast he offered to do what he sometimes did, and go to the village for the paper. They took the local paper each week, and no daily paper.

"Well now," said Tot, "will you spend for me too?"

"I don't mind," said Bob. "Have you any brass?"

"Just plenty, perhaps," said Tot. He was going into his

pockets and bringing out string and wire and bolts, knives, hooks, small stones, a marble, two clogged keys, a hollow pencil; and at last a purse. From the purse he took out a green sixpence, the only coin in it. He said that he wanted a copy of the local paper for himself, this week.

"Take no notice, Bob," said Grandma. "He can read ours, same as always. What's the sense of two?"

"I know the sense of two," said Tot. "And if I've to get it myself, then I will."

"Bob can get it," said Grandma. "I don't think you want it at all. You did it so that you could pretend that sixpence was your last coin."

"It was," said Tot. "But I've five pounds hidden, so I'm right."

"Enough to leave the country," said Bob; but from the way Tot and Grandma looked at him it seemed that the remark was not funny.

He went down to the village on the bicycle he and Dick shared, and rode it most of the way back. But there was a muscle in his side that was twanging as he rode. He got off and walked the rest of the way.

Tot took his copy of the paper and went up into his room. Grandma looked at the front page of hers, and put it on the dresser for later on. She was making bread again.

"I think Tot had a paper last week too," she said. " I wonder how long that's been going on. He went down for them last week."

It was not clear why Tot wanted the paper, even when he had it. Not long after he had taken it up to his room he brought it out again. It had been opened and folded up again. He carried

75

it down the steps, and threw it into the corner of the stick shed where paper was put for lighting fires. Bob went into the shed, curious about what had happened, and looked at the paper. He opened it, and went through the pages. They seemed unread, and not creased with constant perusal.

A small cutting had been taken from one of the pages. That was all. On one side would have been an advertisement among Public Appointments, and on the other some small news item, ending 'his widow, Mrs Austin, lives at Green House, East Ainger. He also left two daughters and five grandchildren.'

Bob put the paper back, after noticing the page and place. He would be able to check from the copy in the house, and then be able to tell Grandma, so that she knew what Tot was up to.

The Public Appointment was for the post of Cook at an Old Peoples' Home in Durham. The news item reported the funeral of a retired police officer, aged 78. He thoughtlessly began, at dinner time, to mention the stick shed, meaning to bring the talk round casually to newspapers. However, Tot had something in mind about the stick shed as well, and changed the course of the talk. Bob found a sort of blush rising in him after a while, when he looked back on himself and saw that he had been doing something silly to the old man. If Tot wanted them to know why he had bought a newspaper he would have said so. He had only to ask Grandma for her paper when it was finished, and he could have it. So he was keeping something from Grandma, and it would not be fair to let her loose on him.

"There isn't plenty in that stick shed," Tot said.

"You'll have to get some cowlings then," said Grandma. "It's the weather for it, and you've nothing better to do."

Tot thought the weather might have changed by Monday; and Grandma thought they could go up today for the cowlings.

Cowlings are the stalks of heather, or ling, left after the spring burning. The heather is burnt off in March, and the new tender shoots are eaten by sheep and by grouse. But the old woody stalks still stand. If they are pulled out they make stuff for lighting fires. Tot thought there wouldn't be much in the way of cowlings to be got, and ling would have to do. Besides, he said, Grandma had complained all last winter about having to light fires with ling and cowlings, when somebody could have chopped up a little wood.

There was a long argument about that, during which Bob looked at his mind, and concluded it was getting untidy and mischievous, and wanted to make trouble.

After dinner Tot had his bit of a smoke. Dick went out and put a collar on the horse, and tied the sledge on. While he was doing that Grandma, washing up in a black fury about the argument over cowlings and sticks, decided they should have a picnic tea, "like Christians", she said, meaning that she thought it would be an elegant thing to do. She put eggs to boil, and filled the teapot used at dinner with cold water and poured the hard mixture into bottles, for cold tea.

"It'll be dowly stuff, will that," said Tot, darkly.

It was dowly stuff, both weak and bitter, when they came to it on the edge of the moor. They had climbed right up the grass lane, to where it ended in a field, and crossed that field, and on to the allotment beyond, all rough grass and pockets and gutters. At the top of the allotment was the moor gate, where the ling began. But at this edge there was no burnt heather.

They had to climb up further, along the dead track that led to the tower.

"They made the road when they built the tower," said Tot. "They built all the towers at the same time. I was a lad then, and I never saw this one built; but there were others north of this. I know they took one down later, but there's some left still."

"I thought they were castles," said Dick. "Or monuments."

"They're sighting towers," said Tot.

"For sighting enemies, or aeroplanes, or what?" said Bob. "Are they all called sighting towers?"

"They will be," said Tot. "The Water Board built them."

"Claro and Craven," said Bob.

"Claro, just," said Tot. "Craven came in later, and they put up the water rate."

The tower was a strange structure. It was made of two parallel walls, about four feet apart, twelve feet long, and a yard thick. These separate walls went up fifty feet, and joined at the top in an archway. There was no inside to the tower: each part was outside. There was no way to the top. There was no date, name, or apparent purpose. Tot said he did not know what they were for. He had only been a child when they were made, and the builders were Irishmen who came up on the railway each day, and went down on it again at night. There was no railway here, of course, but there had been one, he said, in Vendale, where he had seen the towers building. Perhaps they were to get levels, he thought.

Dick edged his way up between the walls, and held himself ten feet up for a moment, looking northwards, before dropping to the ground with an echoing thud. "I think there's another yonder," he said. "I could just to say see the top of it, about two miles off. Are you coming to look, Bob?"

"You can't get," said Tot. "You can't get over Staddle Moss and Huker Mire. It's all bog and quag and water, and it never clears out dry. It's all sour land, from here over to Vendale, if you're going north, and miles either side to east and west. There isn't any road over yonder."

Grandma stood up. "We'll get our cowling now," she said. "And no more talk."

They found a burnt patch, and gathered the blackened stalks. It was a patch burnt off by the commoners who had rights of grazing. They had rights of gathering fuel too, but not many people bothered to exercise the rights these days, even for the sake of a picnic.

They gathered and pulled, with the stalks coming up knotted with roots, obstinate and rough, taking skin and pinching at flesh. A great deal of labour brought in a small supply of woody stuff; but they had the sledge to fill or it wasn't worth coming; and they filled the sledge. Tot brought out some of his string and hayband and tied the load down. Then they came off the edge of the high top and down to the fringe of the moor, where the ling began to run out into grass, and had their tea, with the sorry tea, and the eggs not cool and not quite hard either.

"When I was a lad," said Tot, settling a crust to soak soft in the corner of his cheek, "we could eat right dainty out on the land. There's a way to do it, if you've mucky hands and don't fancy touching what's to end in your gob. I'd show you, but I can't when there's only this shaffling bread and butter and picnic stuff. They don't give us a bit of bread for our bait like they used to."

"You're ailing nowt on your bread and butter," said Grandma. "You'll have some more tea." Tot obediently held out his cup, and poured the tea into his mouth to help with the softening of the crust.

After tea Tot took the head of the horse and led it. Bob went with him, leaving Grandma and Dick to hold the sledge back with ropes, to stop it getting against the horse's heels.

"Tot," said Bob. "Do you want to be a cook in an old peoples' home?"

"Don't be so fond," said Tot. "You're as daft as a gate."

"It's what you cut out of the paper," said Bob. "I looked."

"You saw there was summat up with your Grandma," said Tot. "There was. We thought she was off, if you hadn't been taken bad. I reckon you looked on the wrong side of the paper, Bob."

"The other side was about a policeman," said Bob. "So why did you cut that side out?"

"That was the bobby that was watching her for so long," said Tot. "Tha knows."

"What for?" said Bob. "I don't know. What do you mean?"

"She helped someone get away that was wanted by the police," said Tot. "Did you never know? And this fellow was in the force, and he never let up, always about the place, plaguing us. So you see, when he died last week she thought she might go home again, for a visit. She never went back, they wouldn't have her, for fear of shame. There was no one would have her."

"Where's home, for her?" said Bob.

"I've said plenty," said Tot. "She's settling back, and we'll leave her to settle. She was the grandest lass there was, when she was young, and it's a bad shame the way she was tret; and mostly by that police fellow."

Bob went forward to open the gate; and when he walked with Tot again Tot talked only about hay.

IX

Bob HAD long ago decided that Grandma ought not to appear at school. He did not mind very much that he would be linked with her in the public's eye; but he could not bear the thought of her being laughed at for her strange clothes; nor would he like her to argue with his teachers, either to their faces or at home later. He knew that she could destroy his impression of other people if she wanted. So whenever there was a notice for her about the Parent-Teacher Association, or Sports Day, or other things that might have brought her to school, he lost it on the way home, or dropped it in the waste paper box at school.

There was a bring-and-buy and jumble sale to be held before the end of June, out of the way of haytime. Because he had thrown away the notices Bob hardly knew about it, until the girls began to stock their desks with cakes and jam and orna-ments. All the boys would have liked their hands in the jam or the cakes, and one or two of the worst ornaments were seized from third formers who were considered too noisy with them. The ornaments were stood on the school wall and pelted with stones until they shattered. One vat-like vase was stood on the edge of the platform during prayers, and by some sixth-form arrangement of string and sticky tape was meant to fall off with a fracturing crash among the prayers. Instead it became caught in the sticky tape, bounced off the floor, and then went gungling and yowing hollowly among the legs of the second form. Members of the staff stared out of the window. The string flickered on the floor and disappeared.

"Strawberry Jam," Judith Chapman was saying, tapping the transparent membrane sealing the top of the jar. There was a pygmy drumming from it. Others were showing lemon curd, or unset marmalade. Bob looked at Strawberry Jam, because Judith's desk was nearest. There was a big label on each jar, and one that was hardly necessary, because strawberry jam is easy to recognize, though perhaps it needs the date.

He knew the writing. He had seen it before. Something in him jumped when he saw it, and the back of his mind understood it first, and then the front of it, and his breath stopped. A blue paper had been covered with that writing, on the side of a hill—no, in the gill, after . . . after what?

The memory came to him again, raw and fresh, as if it had happened that very morning. It was a memory that had not fitted in smoothly with time. It was ten days old, and detached. He could hardly tell where it belonged, or even if it belonged to him. The blue paper sat again in front of his eyes, and he could remember it.

"Judith," he said, "write something down."

"Like heck," said Judith, expecting some trick; but when she saw he was serious, pale, and startled, she took a pencil and opened her rough note book. "R.N.B. ready," she said.

"A danger is past and the watcher is dead," said Bob. "I can share something with you and I can forgive you, so come and see me before I die even if you did let somebody go that murdered somebody. Something about a cousin, and being a baby, and then the danger has gone again, and I do not know what to think. Leave plenty of spaces, I might be able to fill it in later."

Then Bob took the rough note book from her hands and tore out the page. "Sorry," he said, wondering whether he was heard, because there was in his head the noise of the underground water and the moiling of the falls in the gill, and there was in his nerves the knowledge of banging and buffeting, as if he had seen things happen to him, but not felt them: all that he had gone through he was going through again, in disarray, without his body being touched.

Two lessons came and went, and he sat and looked at the board or the teacher, or the floor, while he tried to make a structure out of the mixed impressions that had come crowding back. He was able to sort out a dream from the memories, and to put the memories in order. By the end of the second lesson he had a sensible sequence, of swimming in the water, and floating down the waterfall and being dragged down through an opening under the water, more or less unconscious. He had then come out of the underground place, and gone into a dream; in the dream or in the water he had lost his swimming trunks, and they had been found somewhere else later on. Then he had begun to walk home, and had come across a page of blue paper written in the writing on Judith Chapman's jam labels, and the writing had said what Judith had written for him, more or less. And what it said added a whole dreadful dimension to what Tot had said on Saturday about Grandma and the policeman. She had helped a murderer to escape.

Then Dick had knocked him down and taken the paper away from him and put it in the fire. So it was clear that the blue paper had been part of a letter, a letter to Grandma, and she had read it and lost it, or thrown it in the fire and had it float up the chimney—there had been a big blaze for the bread. And that letter had come that morning, and because of it Grandma had been going away. Where? Who would she visit? Was the writing the writing of her cousin?

Who had been murdered? And who had done it?

By break time Bob had put the memory back in the past, where it belonged. He thumped Judith on the back. "Thanks for writing my essay for me," he said. "It was part of a dream I had."

"Was it?" said Judith. She was about to ask him where he lived, and was it Ravensgill; but there seemed no real reason, even if he did have strange writing to be done for him, to connect him with her own family. Except that his name was White, the name on the letter she had posted for Gran.

"Who wrote your jam labels?" Bob asked.

"Gran," said Judith. "Why do you want to know that?"

"Curiosity," said Bob. "I thought I'd seen it before some-where."

"Perhaps your mother bought a pot of jam last year," said Judith. "She only writes jam labels, usually. That's about all I ever see."

"Where does she live? Wakefield?" said Bob.

"No," said Judith. "With us. Why?" But he did not bother to answer.

So Judith Chapman's grandmother is cousin to Grandma, he was thinking, when there was a general call to play cricket, and he answered it.

The facts of the problem lay about his mind all the rest of

85

the day. He thought he might dream about them at night, but if he did he did not remember.

He went for the cows in the morning, and came down with them without going higher up to wash. The sink would do today. He was determined to ask Tot more about Grandma's secret, and to find out how she had helped a murderer.

The shippon had cool walls and a high light from the sun still low to the north-east. The cows had glowing red backs, or shining black ones. Heat from their bodies seemed to spread from the band of sunshine across their spines. Dick started the engine, and it began to suck. Tot slowly scooped out nuts for the cows in each bus, or stall, and began to wash udders. He was quiet and contented, and looked undisturbable. Bob lifted a question from his mind to his throat, and it stuck there, refusing to come out and be spoken. Bob felt the question die, and swallowed it. He went out of the shippon and walked about in the yard, looking at the mad hens stepping as if they were on the moon and peering from their unrelated eyes.

He questioned himself, and the words formed in his mind as if they were printed: Do I want to know about it? He could not tell whether he wanted to know for himself, or whether he wanted to be told by Grandma or Tot, or whether he wanted no mystery to be hanging about him. Why did Dick not want to know? Or did Dick know? Is it always right to find things out, to let things be remembered? And what had it to do with the Chapman family?

He turned the questions round in his mind, framing and forgetting, reframing and remembering them, until he had some sort of solution. He reasoned that if those at Ravensgill wanted him to know they would tell him; and that if Grandma had never said anything about it it was because she did not want to; and the same was true of Tot. He could not tell about Dick. The chief question, and it was a new one, that came to him was about his grandfather. No one had ever said anything at all about him. He had never been mentioned at all. Bob could not even recall his name. But everyone has a grandfather somewhere.

Then he felt guilty for wanting to know; and just as guilty for not knowing. But the problem could not be solved just by thinking about it. He would have to ask someone.

Grandma put her head out of the kitchen door and asked whether all you good people were coming, because she was in a tiresome smiling humorous hostess mood, probably being someone else, like the queen; or like a little girl pretending to be the queen and not knowing much about courtly manners.

Bob let the cows up the lane, and came for breakfast.

During prayers at school he knew what to do, and the obvious person to ask. He had been practising questions to all sorts of people, like Mick Chapman, and even Judith; but the imaginary answers were never any good. He daydreamed into one about asking Mr Lankester, who marched about saying "Swim for it, White, swim for it," and then blew a whistle. From that he thought of the postman, and then of a total stranger who turned out to be his grandfather. Then, as prayers were ending, he thought of the other clue, the policeman. He could only imagine, at the moment, talking to the one that had died; and he thought he would not have done that in any case, because of the danger, whatever it was, that had died with him. But down in the town there were live modern policemen at the police station, and they could tell him.

He knew that sometimes policemen do not tell; but that was not enough to put him off the idea. He laid his plans before dinner time, by asking a boy called Huby whether his father, who was the sergeant at the station, would be at the station in the afternoon. Huby took the enquiry home when he went for his dinner, and brought the answer that his father would be in the office if Bob wanted to go down after school. So by the beginning of afternoon school the rest of the day was fixed. He had to go to the police, and when he went he would have to ask the questions he had thought of, because there was nothing else he could ask.

He walked down into the market place, and then across to the police station, with questions ready. It would be easier to ask someone he knew slightly, even if it was only by being the father of someone else, than to ask someone he knew well. He went up the steps, and as he went up each one the questions seemed more impossible.

Sergeant Huby was in the back office. The constable on duty led him through, and their feet clopped on the green lino. Sergeant Huby was typing. He nodded, finished a sentence, and then came to Bob and sat on the edge of the table.

"Sit you down," he said, prodding a chair with his foot. "Your name's White, isn't it?"

"Robert White," said Bob.

"Where are you from?" said the sergeant.

"Ravensgill," said Bob.

"Oh aye," said Sergeant Huby. "Right up there. You couldn't come from much further away, could you?"

"Not in that direction," said Bob.

Sergeant Huby laughed. "That's a good answer," he said. "I

deserve that." Bob said he hadn't meant anything by the answer, and the sergeant said it was all the better an answer for that. "But what can we do for you?"

"I'm not sure," said Bob.

"There's something bothering you," said the sergeant, "or you wouldn't be trembling and breathing so shallow; but you don't look as if you'd been up to mischief, so you've nothing to worry about; and I'm in no hurry."

"I'm trying to find something out," said Bob. "And I don't like to ask them at home, and I thought you would know, because there was a policeman watching Grandma, but he's died."

"Now, who's your Grandma?" said the sergeant. "All that name and address and so on."

Bob told him. "Lizzie for Elizabeth," said the sergeant. "And now what about the policeman that's died? I don't re-collect anything recent about that."

"It was last week, I think," said Bob. "That's how I got to know there was something funny. It was in the paper."

The sergeant sent out to the office in front for the local paper, and Bob located first the Public Appointments, and then the cutting on the other side. "Him," he said, pointing to it without reading it again.

"Ah," said the sergeant. "There's policemen and policemen, you know; and what's more, this one had retired, had Mr Austin, and he was in another division. I think he was here once, but a very long time ago, something like forty years. He was pretty old when he died."

"Seventy-eight," said Bob. "I remember that."

"I'll find out when he was here," said the sergeant. "I'll look in the establishment book, if it goes back that far."

The book did not go back far enough. It had been started afresh thirty-six years before, and there was no one called Austin on the strength then.

"That's not a lot of help," said the sergeant. "You know, I think you're asking about things that happened too long ago. No one here will remember them."

"I thought you wrote everything down," said Bob. "I got written down when I came in, and you've put my name down since I came in here."

"It isn't every piece of paper that lasts for ever," said the sergeant. "But I'll see if there was a case about your Grandma, if you like. Are you sure you want to know?"

"Yes, please," said Bob. "It was a murder case, you see."

"Murder? At Ravensgill?" said the sergeant. "Well, I can tell you straight off that there's nothing on the books about that. I never heard of it."

"I'm sure there was one," said Bob. "I've heard of it."

"There aren't so many murders up here that I'd forget about one, even forty years ago," said the sergeant. "But I'll go and ask them in the back. They've been here longer than me."

He opened the door between his office and the front office, so that the constable could watch both rooms, and went through into the back of the building. When he came back he had a folder in his hands. "I've dug something up," he said, "but it isn't quite what you say. But I'm afraid I can't tell you, because, though it's so long ago, the case hasn't been closed. My advice is to forget about it, because there's nothing you need worry about; and if Mr Austin was here I'm sure he would close the case and finish."

"Is it something very bad that you can't say about?" said Bob.

"It's bad enough," said the sergeant, "concerning the death of Abraham Dinsdale, about forty-six years ago, in suspicious circumstances. The police began to look into it, but were unable to complete their investigations. That's all."

"Abraham Dinsdale," said Bob. "But who murdered him?"

"I never said anyone did," said the sergeant. "And there's no one suspected of it either. So do what I said: go home and forget about it."

X

EAST AINGER was twenty-three miles away. The first part of the journey tended downhill, as the dale fell away to the plain. The second part was the switchback before the plain began, and the last part was among the flat fields and still rivers of the Vale of York. Under the bridges the water was greasy.

The sun was solid all the way there, and to bicycle under it was like carrying an extra weight. Bob grew drier and drier as the morning turned under his wheels. He had set off for East Ainger to see Mrs Austin, that was the widow of the policeman who had watched Grandma. Since the living police had been no help to him, he thought that perhaps the dead might help. He had the address in mind: Green House.

East Ainger was a village built round a pasture, or green, with a pond and geese grazing. The village hung off the road, and in it nobody stirred, no gate swung, no smoke moved, no voice spoke. Bob cycled slowly round the road that circled the pasture. All the houses were on his right as he went. He read their names, or their numbers. At the far end of the pasture there was a gap among the houses and a big ornamental gate. He saw no number on the gates, and went on to look at the other houses, on the south side of the pasture.

There was no Green House. A picture came into his mind of

people living under glass, with tomatoes and chrysanthemums about them. Then he came back to where he had begun; and he knew he had to ask.

People were watching him now, without really taking notice. He cycled to a garden gate and asked over it where the Green House was. He was told that it was behind the ornamental gates yonder. He went up and cycled through, and was in a drive overhung with trees.

He came on to the side of a house, round a corner, moving out of the shade into the hammering sun again. All here was as still as the village outside. He leaned the bicycle against the house, and went looking for a door.

Before he found one he came upon the lawn of the house, stretching flat to the far hedge, and half-trimmed. At the place where the cutting had ended there was a motor mower in pieces. Bob stepped over it, to see what the pieces were. He saw that the machine was nothing but an engine like the milking machine at Ravensgill, with a number of fancy cowlings and covers to direct the flow of cooling air. He thought it was a simple mechanism, and that it would be easy to make one if there had been a lawn at Ravensgill.

But he had not come here to look at motor mowers. He left it and went looking for the door of the house.

There was a big front door with a dark hall beyond it. The door was open, and on a coloured rug inside a fat white dog lay and wagged its tail at him slowly five times, and then laid its head on its paws and took no notice.

All was so silent (and the dog should have barked) that Bob hardly liked to knock on the door. He looked for a bell, in the hope that that would be softer, but there was none. If he could have heard somebody, he thought, how much easier it would be to make the next noise.

He made the noise. He lifted his fist and dropped it on the panel of the door.

The white dog that had ignored him stood up and roared at him. Along the hall inside the house four doors opened and people came out and looked at him. On the staircase landing at the far end there appeared other figures. In three seconds from touching the door he found himself facing seven people and the dog. The dog went on roaring, and all seven people were shouting at it, and the noise was like the noise of the hunt in full trail. Bob stepped away from the door and stood in the path outside, rather to one side, to let the noise escape past him. The noise died down, and a man came outside.

He said: "My God, what a racket; or have you said that already?"

"Near enough," said Bob. "I came to see Mrs Austin."

"I'm afraid she's away at the moment," said the man. "I'm her son-in-law. Can I help you at all?"

"I wanted to see her about something that happened a bit ago," said Bob. "They wouldn't tell me at the police station in Garebrough, and I thought she might know."

"Mrs Austin's in York," said the man. "Are you going that way?"

"How far is it?" said Bob. The man thought it would be about thirty-five miles. Bob said it was too far, because of getting back home again. Then the man found out from him where he had come from, and on what bicycle.

"I don't like to send you back just like that," said the man. "And it wouldn't be fair, because we're going to see the old lady this afternoon, and we could take you, if you don't mind hanging about until then. And if you can mend the motor mower, you can have the delightful treat of mowing the rest of the lawn."

Bob thought he could mend the motor mower, and he did. There was nothing wrong with the ignition or the mixture; but there was no power to it, and every time the throttle was opened and the clutch engaged the engine would die away to a feeble mutter. Bob listened and felt carefully for a blown gasket, but they were firm enough. It was a four-stroke machine, just like the milking machine, and he felt the compressions, suspecting a burnt valve. But they seemed to be in order. Then he thought of a simple thing that had once gone wrong at home, and looked at the oil level. There was no oil in the sump. He reported it to the man, and between them they toured the three garages of the house, where there were three big cars, and found a pint of oil. Bob poured it into the sump, started the engine, let it run, and found that power was restored. He finished cutting the rest of the grass.

He wheeled the machine round to the garages, where its place was, cleaned the grass from it, and left it there. He went back to his newly-mown lawn and sat on it. There was nothing to do, and nothing to hear.

A fly came singing along the air, looked into each of his eyes in turn, and flew on, out of sight and out of hearing. A church clock in another village struck off mid-day. The garden stood still and bright in front of his eyes like the scenery of a stage.

The fly seemed to have come back unheard, and to have landed on his neck, below his right ear. He flicked it away. It came round to the other side of his neck; and when it was discouraged from there it changed again. After another hint it left. Then it came back on both sides at once, which seemed unnatural of it, even if there were two. It landed on the back of his neck as well, and that was too much for Bob. He got up and waved his arms about, hoping to frighten it, or them, away altogether.

He saw, sitting a yard behind him, close together, three little boys. They had tickled him with long stems of grass. They looked at him, and then they looked at each other. All three had the same looks, but they were different sizes, so they were not triplets. Without a word to each other, and all at once, they stood up, and advanced on Bob with their outstretched grass stems. Bob thought they were uncanny, and retreated in front of them. They dropped their formation of side-by-side, and surrounded him with linked arms. They still said nothing. Bob appreciated that there was a game going on, and joined in it, moving where they wanted him to move.

They moved him round the lawn as they wanted. They began to bully him at last, pinching with small fingers just above his elbows, and dabbing their grass stems at his eyes. Bob wondered if they were elves, or other creatures not known in the hills but common in the plain. He let them pinch him, and he let them punch him, because they did not hurt. When they began to kick he pushed them over, and that was their game for a time. All at once they ran away, leaving him alone. They were back in a moment, running silently on the grass, bringing a ball and a stick. They threw him the ball, and one of them stood in the middle of the lawn with the stick, ready to play French cricket.

Other people began to come out of the house. First was the

man Bob had already spoken to. "Ha," he said, "let's break some legs," and he rolled the ball mildly towards one of the little boys, who lifted the stick too early, and was bowled out. After the man came two women, another man, two rather old ladies, a woman with a sort of nursing uniform carrying a baby, and an old man with a walking stick, and two more children. All except the baby played French cricket. Even the nurse person, who was called Nanny by everyone, or sometimes Nanny Jackson, or even plain Jackson when she broke the rules, joined in. When she did the baby was handed to someone else.

After a long time it was one o'clock, and the game stopped.

"Time for lunch, I vote," said the man Bob had had dealings with before. "This is someone to see Granny, Bob White," because he had taken Bob's name from him when they were looking for oil for the mower. Bob was introduced to the members of the party, without remembering any names at all, even the old man with the stick's name did not stay in his mind. All he knew about him was that he was Lord somebody.

He washed his hands free of oil in a little place under the stairs. He came out into the empty hall again, and nearly walked out and went away, because the day was being so strange and unlike the rest of life. He had mistaken something somewhere, he thought, because a policeman's widow would be an ordinary person, not one having a large house, several huge cars, and a Lord staying there.

Lunch was at a long bright table covered in flowers and glass and knives, spoons and forks with rich silver handles. The baby did not come to the table.

He began to worry about his table manners after he had

begun to eat. In the same way that what would do for school would not do for home, what would do for home might not be right for this house and company. If he had been Tot he would have complained about something, in the way that Tot had complained about bread and butter and picnics in general. Tot would have eaten everything on the plate with a knife, with his left thumb for assistant. No sense in starving, though, he thought, and went on as he had begun, just trying to keep his mouth shut when he chewed.

He saw that the three little boys, sitting in a line on the other edge of the table, were watching him, and copying all his movements. He was not the only one to have noticed. When he teased the little boys by eating several empty forkfuls and drinking an empty glass of water twice, they had to do the same, solemnly. He felt the rest of the company laugh, not at him, but at the little boys. That made them stop imitating.

After the meal Bob was taken to York. He went in the back of one of the big cars, sitting next to the two rather old ladies. In front sat the Lord, and the man Bob had first met drove.

In York they went to a flat, where a little bright old lady sat watching cricket on television. Bob was left with her, and the others went off. The little old lady turned off the cricket, and was friendly. Bob found that she was interested in him, and wanted to know about him. The people in the house at East Ainger had let him in, told him to stay, and then done nothing personal for him at all. He had been left to himself. The old lady, who was Mrs Austin, found out his name, address, school, ambition, name of brother, weight, height, favourite subjects, best sport, and then asked him what he wanted.

Bob began to explain that he wanted to know about something her husband had been doing forty-six years ago. "Our man Tot read that your husband was the policeman that was watching my Grandma," he said. "But no one will tell me what it was all about, and I know it was something bad, even though they told me at Garebrough that it wasn't really anything. It was murder and not murder."

"Forty-six years ago," said Mrs Austin. "He would have been a constable then, I suppose. When I married him he was an inspector, and when he retired he was Chief Superintendent. I'm afraid I can't tell you anything about his time in Garebrough, Robert, and police officers look at a great many people who aren't used to it. The officer makes a note in his book and that's all; but the person looked at often remembers it all his life."

Bob thought that was fair and true. People looked at policemen, but people looked in shop windows, rather than see so many faces.

They sat and talked, and she made a pot of frail tea, and they turned on the cricket again. Bob watched the cricket, and watched the old lady, and was sure that the two things were both imaginary, and that he was not really in York at all, and perhaps did not exist in the usual sense of the word.

He did not come back to his own existence until he had been taken back to East Ainger by the man, travelling alone this time, because the two old ladies and the Lord had been left in York, and was on his bicycle leaving the village. He last saw the three little boys carrying one of the other children about and dropping her in among the roses. Bob left without noticing too hard.

XI

THERE WAS A sense of iron on iron: the bus grinding up the hill beyond Garebrough. A cyclist might have moved faster, Bob thought. But the cyclist would not have been dry, because outside there was that cold rain of summer turning skin blue and washing the bloom off the drying hayfields. The weather had struck chill to Grandma's soul as it gathered the day before and blotted the sun up. She had lived the evening and the night on the thought of coming this journey today.

Bob liked the business and the change of coming with her to Skerne Bank. It was out of the county and out of the next county too, because they left the West Riding, crossed the North Riding, and went into County Durham. He could remember the long voyages by bus to Wakefield long ago, and how the smoke of the towns on the way had seemed to him a sanctified smoke, a reek like incense, part of the offertory of his existence.

The iron on iron grew to sparking intensity. There was a suspension of the intensity, a jerk, and the bus was travelling more gently, but faster, on the downhill slope.

"When that bank's done, then we're three parts through," said Grandma. "This is a journey that's always long enough."

"It's not like going to Wakefield," said Bob. "That was different. But I like going to Skerne Bank."

"It isn't such a change as going there to stop for a day or two," said Grandma.

Lately Bob had been despising Grandma for the journey she used to take. He had often gone with her, and liked it, but he had never had the same electric, urgent purpose in travelling. Now, in this bus, he felt something of what made Grandma travel. Last week he had been to York. This week it was Skerne Bank. Travelling seemed suddenly the only way of filling up Saturdays. However, the mood soon passed, when the shallow Skerne Bank sun began to mark the road. Now he thought that he should be in the field with the hay. Very likely there was nothing to do; but possibly Dick and Tot were turning it.

Tot had begun to cut on Tuesday morning, being out very early, but even then not the first, he said, because he had heard them cutting down below in Gatestead lands. He had started in the field called Skyre Howe, mowing the outside half before his breakfast, and the middle after it, leaving the little hill in the middle with a topknot of standing grass. He had walked down with a scythe later and cut the top-knot down. Bob had cycled down to school past the field, through the sap-laden air as fresh as water. In the evening he had come back up the hill and the same air was resinous with the balsam of the killed blades.

With the first cutting the weather had gone. The next morning had been slow to wake, and the sun had not come until the afternoon. All the same the grass had been ripe, and it had had to be cut. On Thursday they took Skyre Howe into the building, "as good as you'll get, this hay," said Tot. Friday had been a slow day to begin with, and then had chilled; and today was wet with drifting drizzle.

Skerne Bank had wet town roads, but the sun struck randomly among the buildings. The first call was for a cup of coffee, while Grandma studied the cinema posters and wonddered how to arrange the day if they went to a film.

Bob watched her, and waited, and played with the tan skin on his cup of coffee, wrapping it like a shawl over the back of the teaspoon, until Grandma tapped his hand in reproof, an action that made him happy.

When they had set off from Ravensgill Grandma had been strangely dressed, compared with what Bob expected from local people. Her headscarf was wrong, somehow, because she tied it differently from everyone else, and because it was too bright. Her coat was too green, as well as being all picks and pills from old age. She had looked dressed up out of the fashion, and no more. But now, in town, she looked only countrified, not out of fashion or even shabby, but like a visitor. This was the homely Grandma that Bob loved and liked to be with, where her excitement at being in town filled up all the space of her natural nervousness, so that she had no space to turn her energy into rage or malice or even that uncomfortable close guessing that she would accidentally use so often. It was the close-guessing that hurt people most, where she would hit on explanations without having a reason, stab with the blade of knowing and then strike with the fist of suspicion, and leave Dick, or Bob, lying paralysed on the floor of guilt.

It was all gone in town. Here she was so unknown to the town itself that nothing mattered between her and it, and she had no impression to make. She and Bob were on the same side.

They decided to go to the pictures after an early dinner. Bob was not very interested in a romantic film, but he was prepared to sit through it and try to remember the words of the songs, so that Grandma could sing them on the way home. They went down for their dinners with the taste of coffee still in their mouths. On the way they had to stand on the corner of a street while the traffic lights stared the wrong colour at them. There was the window of an office close by, and Bob looked into that. In the window was a dusty display of newspapers, because the office was that of the local paper. Part of the display was a newspaper of 1895 with its florid black title at the top of the page. Beside it were samples of later titlings, up to the present one. Grandma looked with him.

"Well," she said, "I thought they never changed that part of the paper; but they have done plenty of times since I started to read it. Do you think they keep all the old copies?"

When they were having dinner he told Grandma that he did not want to go to the pictures, but he would meet her when she came out, if she liked.

"Keep off the line, that's all," said Grandma, thinking that he was going to the station to watch the trains. "And don't bother to wait for me, but go back when you want. I might want to see the film through twice if it's a good one." In fact Grandma was capable of staying in the cinema from twelve noon until half past ten at night, and she had done once, in Wakefield.

"I might not go to the station," said Bob.

"You're big enough and ugly enough to do what you like," said Grandma. "I'll give you your bus fare and the pictures money, and a bit more, and then you can do what you like, same as I am. It's just nice to get away from that old farm for a bit."

Grandma went to the first house. Bob walked down to the traffic lights and looked in at the newspaper office window again. Then he went into the office.

The hall of the building smelt of ink and warm paper, a smell not quite sour. There was a girl at an opening in the wall, like a ticket office opening. Bob remembered that Grandma was probably at this moment buying her cinema ticket. The girl smelt of ice cream, or lipstick.

"Yes, honey," she said. "Do you want something?"

"Do you keep all your old copies?" said Bob.

"We don't light the fire with them," said the girl. "You want to be down the passage, there, and that end door on the left, you know, this hand (and she waved her right hand) going along."

"Aye," said Bob. "On the right."

"Saucy, aren't we?" said the girl. "Ask for Mr Moulas. But it's a job to remember which hand's which with so many, isn't it?"

"Well, ta," said Bob.

"Welcome," said the girl.

Bob tapped on the door at the end of the passage, on the right. There was a cry from within, that might mean anything. It was repeated, and Bob opened the door and walked in.

A man with glasses was sitting at a table smoking. He had smoked so much that the room was darkened with the fumes, both the walls and the paint and the air. Bob pushed his way into the stacked still layers, and suspended particles started to dry his throat. The man went on with what he was doing, sticking papers together with a paste that smelt of marzipan.

"Shan't be a moment," he said. "There, that's got it in shape. Now, what shall I do for you?"

"I wanted to read some old papers," said Bob.

"How old?" said Mr Moulas. "We go back to 1832, but there's a few missing early on."

Bob calculated back, subtracting 46 from the present year, and suggested the year he had arrived at and the one preceding and the one following, because the term 'forty-six years ago' is not very exact.

"We can do that," said Mr Moulas. "When do you want to see them?"

"Can't I see them today?"

"Oh yes, you can start," said Mr Moulas. "But you've got twelve volumes to look at, because there's a fresh one every six months, and at the date you're wanting there were two papers, quite separate, and we have two sets, quite different too. In fact we can do you four sets, if you want both areas."

Bob asked about areas, and found that one was Yorkshire, and the other Durham. He settled for Yorkshire.

A quarter of an hour later he was in an upstairs room with a view over the railway, with twelve huge volumes stacked on a table.

"No disfiguring," said Mr Moulas. "And it's all copyright, so don't go printing it without asking."

Reading was awkward. There was a stand, set sloping, where the volumes would rest; but the thicker side of the open pages would slide down and have to be held up in place with one hand, and towards the middle of a volume both sides would have to be held, and that meant holding his hands at the most uncomfortable angle there was, rather at waist level, fingers up and palms flat, just where they will not go flat. He had to take the first volume off the stand and lay it on the table, then kneel on the chair and read it from above.

He planned his work. He would look through the papers of one breed until he found something useful, and then he would go straight to that edition of the other breed, and read what it said there. It meant that when he had scanned the first volume and found nothing, that he could put its parallel copy aside too.

Each volume took some time, even when he only read the headlines. He was looking for 'death' and 'police' and 'murder', 'Ravensgill' or 'serious' or 'charge'.

He found it in the third volume, late June of the year that was forty-six in the past.

INQUEST ON VENDALE FARMER
Ravensgill death

'After the body of a Vendale man, Mr Abraham Dinsdale (47), had been found in a battered condition in Ravensgill a search was immediately made for his assailant, said Police Constable Austin, of Garebrough at the inquest on Wednesday. The Constable said that a message was telephoned to the Police Station at 7.25 p.m., and that he had immediately proceeded to Ravensgill, arriving there at thirteen minutes past eight, when he had viewed the body, now known to be that of Mr Dinsdale. It had been considerably bruised and the skin broken and it had been in the water. After a search Mr Clifford Patrick White, an Irishman, and the owner of the farm at Ravensgill, had been seen, at approximately half past eight, and had been questioned.

'Mr Thomas Tuker, labourer, said that he had found the body at approximately half past six, or within five minutes. Mr Dinsdale had been his employer. They had both come across to Ravensgill because Mr Dinsdale wished to speak to Mr White. Mr Tuker had come to act as witness in case there was trouble. Mr White had not been in the farm when they arrived, and Mr Dinsdale had gone up the gill a little way to see whether Mr White was there. Mr Tuker fully expected that there would be trouble. He had not seen Mr White until about half past eight, when he had come down the gill acting normally, that is, whistling.

'The Police Surgeon said that death had been caused by shock to the heart. Although the body had been in the water there was no sign of drowning. It was his opinion that the deceased had been brutally manhandled with injuries including a fractured skull, but that the fractured skull had not been the immediate cause of death, which was heart-failure after a sudden exertion. He thought that the exertion must have been extraordinary, because the deceased was a farmer accustomed to heavy work. It was possible that fear had been a factor.

'Evidence of identification was given by Elizabeth Dinsdale, daughter of the deceased. However, when the Coroner had begun to address the jury and instructed them that various verdicts were open to them, including that of Murder by an unknown person or by any known person, Miss Dinsdale interrupted and asked to give evidence again. The Coroner then said she might give additional evidence, and she asked to be sworn in again. The Coroner pointed out that since she was already sworn reswearing was unnecessary. Miss Dinsdale then declared that since her earlier evidence of identification had been compatible with her being Miss Dinsdale she had not revealed to the court that she was in fact married to Mr Clifford Patrick White, and that for the next part of her evidence she wished to be known as his wife. The Coroner allowed her to be sworn again, and took again her evidence of identification, and further evidence, that from about half past four on the afternoon in question Mr White had been in her company in her father's house in Vendale, until rather after seven o'clock, when he had left.

'The Coroner then concluded his remarks to the jury, who, after retiring, brought in a verdict of wilful Murder against Clifford Patrick White, of Ravensgill. The Coroner refused to accept their rider that Mrs White (Miss Dinsdale) had committed perjury, which was, he said, a matter for another court.'

Bob read that twice, and then looked for it again in the other paper. He found it all written down in much the same manner, but he read that version twice as well. He thought then that he must have seen all there was. After that, he assumed, Clifford Patrick White was taken away and hanged. His own grandfather.

He looked at the railway for a moment or two, and closed the volume he was on. Then he wanted to read it again, and he pulled open the back cover. There, in a later issue, was another heading:

RAVENSGILL SUSPECT ESCAPES
Handcuffed man free
'Clifford Patrick White, who was arrested in Vendale on Wednesday night last week after the Coroner had made out a

warrant for his apprehension, escaped almost immediately, said Garebrough police on Thursday. Constable Austin and Sergeant Fireclough had proceeded to Ravensgill farm in search of the accused man, and had then, not finding him there, gone to his wife's house in Vendale, where he was taken into custody in his wife's presence. His wife, formerly Miss Elizabeth Dinsdale, daughter of the murdered man, then collapsed and while Constable Austin attended to her the accused leapt from the window and ran off in the darkness. The two officers instigated a search, but were unable to come upon any trace of White. They returned to the farm and Mrs White accompanied them to Garebrough Police Station, where she remained the night. The magistrates in the morning said that while they sympathised with the police view that Mrs White had obstructed them in the course of their duties, they could not find it proved that she had deliberately fainted, and nor could she have anticipated the fact that Constable Austin would leave the room in search of a stimulant for her, and they could not find evidence of complicity between her and her husband. Mrs White was found not guilty.'

Mr Moulas came in then, and found Bob reading and re-reading the paragraphs.

"You all right?" he said. "You look as if you've found something nasty."

"I have," said Bob. "I'm not sure. I can't tell yet."

"It can't be that bad," said Mr Moulas. "Forty-six years ago, the population of the world's changed almost completely by now."

"Some are still alive," said Bob.

"And the rest of us are going home now," said Mr Moulas. "So I have to put the books away."

"I've finished," said Bob. "When do they hang people?"

"After the murder," said Mr Moulas. "There's a trial first, of course, judge and jury, and so on."

"What about the Coroner?" said Bob. "Isn't that the jury too?"

"Inquest finds the cause of death," said Mr Moulas. "The jury sometimes thinks it knows who did the murder, if it was one, and then the Coroner has to issue a warrant to the police to arrest him, but there's still a trial after that."

"Unless he escapes," said Bob.

"They could always try someone else," said Mr Moulas. "For a change."

XII

"COME DOWN to the reservoir, Judith," said Mick. "I want to
show you something."

"Tell me first," said Judith. "And then."

"You have to see it," said Mick. "Leave your homework."

Gran agreed about leaving the homework. "It's no place for
a healthy girl, isn't the inside of a book," she said. "I don't
think you get about enough for a young girl, Judith. You're a
bit fat."

"Come on, fat," said Mick. "Run it off down the road."

Standing beside the reservoir was like standing in a warm
dish recently filled with cold milk. There was a coolness rising
from the water, and heat pulsing out of the land. The drizzle
of the weekend had done nothing to lift the level of the water;
and it had probably lowered itself rather than been raised.
Now it was evening, and the sun was pouring into the end of
the valley from west and north. Down below the dam there
had been shadow. Up here there was brilliant light, and the
sun sinking but still high over the hills.

Mick changed in the bushes, and then skipped down to the
water. He stood at the edge for a little, looking round the edges
of the reservoir. Then he chose his place to enter the water,

went in, shook his head back, and started to swim in a certain direction, now and then stopping to splash and check where he was.

He went some distance out, then stopped for a longer time, and cast about him, looking for something.

"It's floated away," thought Judith.

Mick found it. He ducked under water, and then did not reappear swimming, but climbed out of the water and stood up, his full height. He was standing on the water.

Then he swam back. "What do you think to that?" he said, coming out of the water.

Judith had been amazed, and shocked, and worried. "I think it's blasphemous," she said. "Only Jesus is meant to walk on the water, and I don't think you should, even if you can. What else can you do?"

"You are as soft as a brush," said Mick. "There's just a rock there, or summat, and I stood on it, that's all."

"I still think it's wrong," said Judith. "You shouldn't do things that remind other people of things that you shouldn't be doing."

"Daft isn't the word," said Mick. "I don't know."

They had finished haymaking for that day. There was nothing to do until next morning, when another field would be ready to bale. Mick had stayed off school several times during the week, because he was in his last three weeks there, and was not worried about any report that might appear in his record, because his employment would be at home, who knew about him in any case. He had become glorious at school by winning the finals of the swimming in freestyle, breaststroke and butterfly, three sorts of diving, and by saving the relay race, which had got into arrears before he swam. The school was first in the Inter-schools championships. So he was doing what he liked with the world, sometimes not going to school but working at home all day and going down to the village at night and coming home late and noisy.

Daddy was leaning on the dam, looking towards the falling sun, when they came up.

"Another day or two, and we'll see the smoke," he said.

"What of?" said Judith. "The moors burning?"

"The old houses," said Daddy. "The reservoir has three houses in it. Mick was standing on the chimney of Scar House, which was the house of our farm before they built the new one we have now. If the water gets much lower we'll see the chimney above the water, and I was just remembering from when I was a lad and the water dropped so low we walked out to the building and lit a fire in the fireplace, for a remembrance."

"What a do," said Mick. "Judith thought I was doing a miracle."

"I didn't," said Judith. "I thought you were pretending to do a miracle, by miraculous means, which is wicked."

"There's Scar House," said Daddy. "And higher up but lower down, if you see what I mean, there's High Ings. It's higher up the valley, but lower down the side. And right at the top there was Snare Gill, but they pulled that down. My father came to Scar House just before it was taken over. Your Gran was from Snare Gill, which her father had, Joseph Dinsdale. And at High Ings there was his brother, Abraham."

"Gran's uncle," said Judith. "Is that where her cousin lived, that you don't talk about?"

"That's where her cousin lived that we don't talk about," said Daddy. "Now be off in."

Mick was angry with Judith now, for mentioning what she had been told to forget. It seemed that he knew more about it now than Judith. All the way home he would not allow her to speak at all, and walked behind her flicking the backs of her knees with his damp towel. It was stingingly painful, and she was crying when she got home, because he would not stop. When he was angry he continued relentlessly, using small punishing vengeances, until something got in the way of stopping him, or he went right on into a destructive rage.

Mother stopped him this time, and took the towel away. Mick went out again and could be heard clattering cans. Judith sat on the floor and tried to see the backs of her knees. She thought her legs were perhaps plump; and an ugly red.

"We'll have a cup of tea," said Mother. "Just run upstairs and pull the curtain across on the little ones. It's time they went to sleep."

Judith felt better when she had come down from that task. She had rattled the curtain across, slapped one little one, shaken the other, kissed both, and left a satisfactory silence behind her.

Gran was sitting in the other room, where she always crept in the evening, saying that if she had finished being useful she would keep out of the way. Judith took her a cup of tea, which she regarded as a scandalous luxury, and took, chuckling naughtily.

"Cup of tea is what I need," said Judith, when she was back with Mother, sitting on the rug by the fire and leaning against Mother's legs, and one of the cats walking one foot on her leg, wondering whether to climb up on Judith's flat lap.

"It's grand to be able to sit down with it," said Mother. "Instead of carrying drinkings and allowances and I don't know what out to the fields all hours. They were still faffing about in Holly Banks at eleven last night; I don't know how they could see."

"Mick shouldn't go to bed so late," said Judith. "It makes him bad-tempered."

"He fires up easily anyway," said Mother. "And he's getting up to boyish tricks in the village at night, drinking better than shandy, I shouldn't wonder. But I'll catch him one of these nights. What was he whipping you for just then?"

"I was just asking Daddy about that thing you won't tell us," said Judith. "But you will tell me, won't you, because I've got to know, haven't I?"

"You haven't, you know," said Mother. "We'd have got it out of the way and forgotten if Wig hadn't spoken out like that. So don't you go pestering us about it."

"You're all like that," said Judith, sitting up. She did not say any more about it, because when she sat up she hit Mother's saucer with her head, and Mother's cup came down full of tea in front of her face, landed right way up with a clunk in Judith's cup, and tipped all the liquid out over the cat, that was settling on her waist.

Judith and the cat stood up together. The cat finished on the floor with both cups, a saucer and a spoon rattling round its head, while Judith tried not to tread on it. Then it jumped on to the table and licked one wet shoulder, and four wet feet, because most of shower had missed it. Judith was the wet one. Mother would not take it seriously at all, and lay back in her chair laughing, waving a saucer and a spoon. Judith stamped off to bed, shouting that Mother could see to her clothes; and as she took off layer after damp layer in the bathroom she threw each garment down the stairs. Mother, at the bottom of the stairs, picked them up, still giggling. They were school clothes, and had to be ready again for the next day.

The next day, at breakfast, Judith laughed about it herself, until Mick, who was in a sour mood at having to go to school, managed to make the rest of them sour too. He was sullen in school, and only began to cheer up on the way home. When he got back he was out into the fields at once, and on to a tractor.

"We'll have to take the tea out," said Mother. "If we can trust each other to carry things." Then they had another giggle about it, and stroked the cat, and giggled again, in front of Gran, who did not like such headless behaviour, and thought they might be laughing at her. The two little ones joined wildly in the giggling without knowing what it was about, and the kettle boiled over and made them all choke.

The next day was Friday. Mick came more happily to school, because after Friday there would be two complete days in the fields if the weather held.

The weather did not hold. By the middle of the day there were clouds, and by the end of school there was rain falling warmly, and a low mist catching on the hill tops. The bus, and then the taxi, climbed higher and higher towards the ceiling of cloud, and then left them at their own gate. Mick went out to survey the fields, and Judith went in.

"You look thoughtful, Judith," said Mother.

"I am," said Judith. "I am very thoughtful. And I'm going to do all my homework tonight, and think all day tomorrow and all day Sunday, and then I might tell you what I've thought."

During the dinner hour, when the second dinner was clattering and shouting in the dining-room, Bob White had come and stood beside her desk. "I think you're my cousin," he said.

"Big deal," said Judith, because she had heard other people say it on hearing grave announcements with no real importance in them.

"It's only a guess," said Bob. "But you know that label on the jam you brought for the parent-teacher thing?"

"Strawberry, and so on," said Judith. "Is that your cousin too?" But she knew what he was beginning to talk about.

"Well, never matter," said Bob. "I'll ask your brother."

"Mick?" said Judith. "No, don't do that, he's furious about it."

"If you know, then it doesn't matter much," said Bob. He had started to talk about it because he could not keep it to himself any longer. He had started to talk to Dick, but Dick had put a friendly hand on his face and pushed him over and said he had heard and forgotten, so shut up. And Tot was so very probably the Thomas Tuker mentioned in the newspaper that it would be wrong to mention it to him: he would speak if he wanted to speak. After them there was Grandma; but she was the least likely person to be talked to. Judith was next. And now she was being silly and indirect about it, so that he did not know whether he was right to speak at all. But she seemed to know.

"I don't know," said Judith. "No one will tell me, and I know there is something, and I expect you are my cousin or some relation like that, because you're White, and my Gran's

117

cousin is a White, I think, and they won't talk about her. Do you know what it is? Why do they let you know and not me? Is it a very bad thing?"

Bob was about to say, dramatically (because when he had read about it, with a little knowledge in front of him, it had been dramatic enough) that it was murder. But Christine Hammerton, Judith's friend, came and sat on her desk and interrupted them, and he said nothing.

"Well, later on, White," said Judith.

"Like that, is it?" said Christine, which was what everyone boringly said if boys talked to girls.

"We're cousins," said Judith.

"Who isn't?" said Christine. "I've eleven cousins in this school, and two more coming next year, and nine more that have been through and left, and more being born every minute."

There was little chance to speak during the afternoon break, and then Bob managed to say very little more, because it was Judith, who knew very little, that did all the talking.

"There was a policeman," she said. "That's all I know. And he was after someone called Lizzie, that was my Gran's cousin, and she wrote to her the other day to tell her the policeman was dead now."

"Mr Austin," said Bob. "I met all sorts of people at his house."

"Wig told Gran," said Judith. "Wig's a man we have. Then Gran wrote to this Lizzie."

"Lizzie is my grandmother," said Bob. "And I read the letter, but I was ill then, and I forgot about it until I saw the writing on the labels. The letter was on blue paper."

"And in a blue envelope," said Judith.

"I didn't see that," said Bob.

"I posted the letter," said Judith. "So I know you come from Ravensgill." They had not known quite how the land lay between Ravensgill and the top of Vendale, and they went to the map that was a faded and permanent fixture in one of the classrooms. It was the 1925 edition, printed in blue and black, and the screws that held the board down and that were under the paper had rusted through. The contour lines, if there were any in that edition, had long since faded, and the blue waterways spread in flat white plains, making each valley with its side valleys like the laid-out veins of a cluster of leaves.

They found the head of Vendale, with its reservoir, and the black square beside it that was New Scar House. To the south they found Ravensgill, and the water there running to join a different river from Vendale's river. Between lay a white expanse called Staddle Hill, Staddle Moss, and Huker Mire; and across the white expanse a busy boundary that was County and Parish and Rural District and Parliamentary. The roads between the two places swung far to the east.

"You can't get across the top," said Bob. "Our Tot says."

"So does our Wig," said Judith.

Then they had to explain Tot and Wig. They came to the conclusion that perhaps they were related to each other, and might be brothers. They compared surnames at last, and found that they were both called Tuker, and that seemed to settle it.

"Now tell me exactly what it is no one else will tell me," said Judith.

"It's a bad thing," said Bob. Now that he had found himself able to mention it to someone, without being rebuffed, he felt he wanted to keep it to himself; and he felt as well that if Judith's family would not tell her, then perhaps he ought not to. By speaking at all he had taken the pressure off his knowledge, and more speaking was not so urgent. But it could be done.

"It was . . ." he was beginning; but Judith seemed to have had a thought process like his own. "No," she said. "Don't say yet. Perhaps I shan't want to know. I'll tell you on Monday whether I want to know. I might not want to. They might be right to keep it secret." And then she ran away from him and started a romping game with Christine Hammerton, a great romper.

XIII

Before Bob slept on Friday night he knew that there was something missing from knowledge. The feeling that something was not there settled against the side of his mind and hindered the flow of his thoughts. There was an incompleteness in what he knew. It was one thing to understand the words of the paper he had read, but another to find their meanings. If Clifford Patrick White had killed Abraham Dinsdale . . . But Bob had gone over that idea many times, and had concentrated his thoughts on Grandma each time, and concluded that, silly as she was, she was not one to tell a big thumping lie. Her lies were all little, unprovable, true ones. The verdict at the inquest had been wrong. Bob was not worried by that part of the story. The part lying next to it puzzled him, because he did not see how Clifford Patrick White, his grandfather, could have come from Vendale, now he knew exactly where it was, over seven miles of road, in the short time he said he had. There must be a way over the top, in spite of what Tot said.

When he went to sleep there was still a nagging thought that the story was unsatisfactory, all pieces, not hanging together. In the morning, stronger than the inadequacy of the story, was the desire to tell it to someone; but no one to tell it to. He got up with Dick and went up for the cows, on a morning that was still wet with rain falling gentle and soft, but certainly falling, not enough to have filled the river at the bottom of the gill, but enough to dampen any cut grass, so that it would have to be turned. There was a lightness in the sky that made sunshine probable later on.

The feet of the cows kissed stone under mud as they went down, and lifted a sigh from the ground as they came up again. Minnie, the last cow, put her tongue in either nostril and plodded after the others. Bob let the rain wash his face, and then went home to the glaring and welcome fire of breadmaking, and let the heat of that pull the damp from his skin.

After breakfast he went out again and found that the sky had lifted and was letting more light through. He went up the lane and across the pasture, and up the track towards the top of the moor. There, he thought, with no one to talk to he might wish to talk to no one. And as well as that there was a strong feeling that since he so much wanted to find a way over the top of Staddle Hill and the Moss, then his desire would show him the way. And he had not only a way to find but a place for it to lead him to.

There was a little wind buffeting the top of the hill. It blew rain into his ears as he went, until he came to shelter, the tower. Here he could see the direction of the rain clearly, where it had blown on a corner and two walls and part of a facing wall and its corner, darkening dark stone and brightening bright green of moss and lichen.

He stood between the walls of the split tower, and looked down the hill behind him. Almost straight down there was the dub where he swam. The little wind was setting from there, and he thought he could hear the water moving in the falls. In the other direction there was the flat Moss itself, and from it came the sounds of sinking and rising water, like a very slow boiling far off. The reeds grew thick over it. He remembered the story of the man who told a secret to the reeds, who told it again to the king. He thought that was a portent, and that he ought not to speak.

When he was last at the tower with Dick, and the rest of the household, gathering cowlings, Dick had racked himself up between the walls of the tower and glimpsed the further tower, or one of the further towers. Bob thought that if he were to venture in to the Moss he might as well have an idea of where the other tower was before he began. He was very nearly the same size as Dick, though not so full of muscle yet. And, he thought, he could see distance better than Dick could, with his rather short sight and glasses. He put a foot on the jutty stones at either side of him, and lifted himself a step or so. He slid down at once, because his shoes were slippery with wet, and so were the stones; and there was in any case a strain on his muscles that he could not bear, since he had to force his feet apart against the walls.

He tried again, this time walking up one wall with both feet and up the other with his back and shoulders. This was a much more successful and secure method, though uncomfortable for back against the face of the stone, and for hands, which had to lift him each pace. Again the worst of the strain was keeping his body stretched enough to touch both walls of the tower at once: one wall would not be enough.

He saw the next tower. He could see right through it, because it was built exactly like the one he was in, and in the same line. It stood there on a distant skyline, like an echo of his present familiar one.

His legs began to tremble, with being so extended. He had to come down. It was easier to see how necessary it was to come down than to come down in fact. He lowered himself a course or two, measuring by the stonework. Then he got his movements wrong, and lost his feet, grabbed at passing stonework, scratched his hands, and landed with a boom on the flat stones at the bottom of the tower, bent his knees, hit the stone with them, rolled over, and stood up. He had not fallen very far, he reckoned; but it had felt further from above because there had been nothing below him, so he had been falling purely down and not over the edge of anything.

He remembered the echoing noise of feet landing on the stones from when Dick had jumped down. He assumed it was the top of the tower that sent the sound down again. He picked up a loose rock lying in the grass, kindly shook off some slugs and small insects clinging to it, and apologised to three worms which stayed a moment in the subterranean tracks that had been roofed by the stone and then pulled away all three at once into their tunnels, as if the light of day took a little time to act on them.

He dropped the stone on to the flags and listened to the noise that came. It was not the roof of the tower that caused the echo, he was sure. There was some sort of hollow under the stone flags flooring the tower. But that was not what concerned him now. He was going to walk across the Moss; not because he was checking on Grandma, but because he knew there must be a way over it.

He left the firm earth and walked on the quaking ooze. After fifteen steps his right leg went in as far as the knee and came out stockinged in black, and a putrescent humour rose from the place where the leg had been. There was no hole: it filled as the leg came up. Bob ran back to the edge and shook the fibrous mould from his calf. That wasn't the way to work it out, he thought. It was no good running straight into a place that is known to be impassable. The silly thing to have done was the starting from the tower, when there was no reason to believe it had anything to do with a way over the Moss. Instead of trying again there he walked eastwards along the edge, looking for likely places.

This way brought him above the farm. He could smell the smoke of it loitering up the hill in the drizzle, and he thought of the fire that made the smoke, and went down to it.

Grandma was kneading the bread, now that it had risen for the first time, and putting it down again to rise in the tins. He sat by the fire to share some of the warmth. Grandma made coffee. Tot knocked at the door and came in, and Dick came for his. Grandma looked at the weather and blamed Dick for it, and Tot for being old-fashioned about deciding when to cut the hay, and then Dick again for being new-fangled about it; and all the time the ungot hay lay damp in the field. Bob sat drying by the fire.

The rain stopped. The bread went in. Grandma put Bob on to peeling potatoes for dinner. Tot went to his own room, saying he might as well sleep as owt else, if there was nowt to do. Dick went out, and down to the village, and bought the paper. Grandma said she would go down later with the order for groceries, with the meaning that she would be glad to get out of the house, but that she wasn't offering to fetch the paper as well.

After dinner the sun came out and glowed small. There was still nothing to be done in the fields. Tot went out and looked at the cut grass, and thought it would be best left to itself. Dick read the paper.

Bob was restless again, unable to sit long in a chair or go anywhere in the farm with purpose, or read, or open his books and do his homework. He picked warm crumbs from the new bread until it was taken away from him. Then he knew that the only thing to do with the day was to go down to Vendale and talk about the inquest and the arrest and the murder.

He took the bicycle and pedalled off down the wet road, with a narrow spray pluming behind him and another jetting forward from the top of the front wheel.

Then he had the long climb into Vendale, up the side of the hill; and then a drop into Vendale itself, and four and a half miles after leaving Ravensgill he was at the head of Vendale, and as far as the county council tarred road went.

He enquired at an abandoned railway station, now a shop, for New Scar House, and was told to follow the railway, and the entrance was pointed out to him. He opened the gate, and began to ride up the ridged track.

The sun unfolded, almost with a sound, like a flower bursting out of bud, and the heat wrapped itself round him like the strong scent of the flower.

The track seemed to be level, but it was heavy going, and hot. He went on for a mile, and then had to stop and draw breath. He wondered what was the matter with him. He wondered too why the river bed below was getting deeper and deeper, when, if he was riding along a level and drawing near the head of the valley, it should be getting shallower.

He toiled on; and came round a corner and saw the dam ahead of him, and the track running up towards it. Now he was aware of a sudden twist in his perception; seeing now that the track was not level but rising, and the valley floor not sinking but lying level. The very gentle slope had misled him. Now he knew he was going uphill all the time, and when he understood his body understood.

He went through a gateway, and was at the top of the railway. On the right was the road over the dam, narrow and straight. Ahead was the reservoir, with the water lying in a pit, having sunk so low. There was another structure against the hill on this side. At first he thought it was another dam, but when he had moved a little way he saw it was a retaining wall, against the hill.

He crossed the dam. Here the sun was shining straight along, and the roadway had dried out. It was like being in the oven with the bread, slabs of heat leaning out from the walls. Far away below water ran in a moderate stream.

At the end of the dam the road turned left and right. The left-hand road went up over the moor. The right-hand one went up a used lane towards a farm. Bob went up towards the farm.

There was a yard, and a back door. Bob put the bicycle against a building, and untucked his trouser legs from his socks, and had a scratch at his warm ankles.

Someone came into the yard. It was Mick Chapman. "Hey, you, White," he said. "—— off."

"What for?" said Bob.

"Because we don't want your lot here," said Mick. "You've been here before and you needn't come again. So get lost."

Judith came to the back door and watched. Mick had a thickish stick in his hand. He thumped the saddle of the bicycle, and it jerked against the wall.

"Now, look out for that," said Bob mildly, because he knew that he had to lose the battle. He was the intruder, and he was not welcome, and there was nothing he could do. He had to go away. The back door slammed. Bob looked at it. Mick did not. He watched Bob. Bob bent to tuck his trouser legs into his socks again, but when he did Mick struck the bicycle again so that it fell over. Bob picked it up, turned his back on Mick, and rode down the beginning of the slope on the pedal, expecting to be struck by the cudgel himself. But Mick was only seeing him off the premises, standing in the yard and swinging his arms.

Bob swung himself on the bicycle, and floated down to the dam. Riding gently along that he blushed, from a sort of shame at not standing and fighting, from relief, and from the heat of the sun. At the end of the dam he stopped, and looked across over the deeps of the valley, to the house on the hillside. He could not see anyone watching him. He looked along the dam to be sure, and then tucked his trousers into his socks, and was ready to go. He did not go in a hurry, but waited for his breath to be ready. Then he let himself drift.

He had not gone far when there was a muted shout, that might have been a sheep, but was not. He put his brakes on and slowed, but did not look round or stop. The shout came again, and he heard that it was his name, White, and knew it was Judith's voice.

She was standing against a hedge by the trackside, and she beckoned to him.

"Did he hurt you? I told you he was funny about it."

"He beat the bicycle," said Bob. "That's all."

"He'll see us here," said Judith. "Come down to the bridge."

The bridge was beyond a steep field, and lay across the river. It was a single-plank bridge with a rail either side, and was in sections like a long V with a hyphen across. It swung and gave as they walked on it. The river was fringed with trees, and the farm from here was out of sight, and the bridge out of sight of the farm.

There were two little girls with Judith, and they played a game across the bridge, shrieking and shouting and making it sway.

"Twins, are they?" said Bob.

"Hand-reared," said Judith. "That's what makes them tame. What did you come for? I was going to think until Monday."

"So was I," said Bob. "But I couldn't wait, I want to tell someone, and I can't tell them there, because they don't talk about it."

"Perhaps I oughtn't to know," said Judith.

"It's nothing indecent," said Bob. "Just interesting."

"I don't know if you should tell me," said Judith. "But they only said they wouldn't tell me, and they didn't say I couldn't know. Start with Lizzie."

Bob leaned on the rail and looked down at the varnish-thin water covering the stones below. He said that Lizzie was his Grandmother, and that her name was White, and she seemed to have married secretly, and she was at her father's house one time when her husband was at his own farm, Ravensgill; or at least, Abraham, who was a great-grandfather to him, and a great-great-uncle to Judith, had thought so, and had gone to look for him there. But something had happened to Abraham at Ravensgill.

"Deaded, was he?" said Judith, decorating the plain word.

"He died," said Bob. Then he explained about the inquest, leaving out the part that was not clear to him about Grandma changing her name part way through and starting again. He said that Clifford Patrick White had been accused of killing Abraham by the jury, and had been arrested, in spite of having a good alibi from his wife.

"They didn't believe her," he said.

"It's the sort of thing my Gran wouldn't believe," said Judith.

"But I know my Grandma," said Bob. "She doesn't do that kind of lie."

"I don't mind about being true or not," said Judith. Then she had to shout at the little ones for something, to clear the air round the point of whether Bob's Grandma had been truthful or not.

"They came and arrested my grandfather," said Bob. "But he got away, with handcuffs on, and I don't think they've ever seen him since."

"Is that everything?" said Judith.

"Yes," said Bob. "Except for one thing . . ." But he said no more, because Mick was on the bridge, advancing on him again, with the same thick stick. Bob stood his ground this time, but Mick came on. He pulled Judith away and off the bridge, and then came towards Bob.

"I told you to —— off," he said. But by then Judith was

screaming in rage, and the two little girls were crying. Mick lowered his stick. "Go on," he said. "Just go. You keep off my family, you, or I'll kill *you* next time. It's our turn."

"It isn't," said Bob. "You don't know the story." But he turned and went. Mick went back to calm the girls down. Then he gave a last shout: "We'll come again. Watch out."

XIV

"It's a shame on such a bright night," said Grandma.

"Bright night, heck," said Dick, looking out of the kitchen door at a festering evening.

"I could play the piano," said Grandma, "and we could have a singaround."

"We'll be off, then," said Dick. "Away, Bob."

"If I could be sure you were going to the pictures and not to Gatestead," said Grandma.

"Might do that and all," said Dick, pushing Bob out through the door and closing it behind them both. "I tell you what, we should have said nowt."

"We could have said we were strowing in one of the gill fields," said Bob. "To save trouble, like."

They went down to the village on the tractor and caught the bus there. As usual, they had to go in during the second picture and come out in the middle of it on the next showing, to get the bus home, or walk ten miles; but it did not matter very much with the films that came to this cinema. When they went in the lights were on, and the audience, not very big, was shouting, because the film had broken and was being spliced. During the big picture the manager had come out on the stage in front of the screen and threatened to close at once if there wasn't better behaviour. The place smelt of beer, and was full of farm lads and town lads and their girls who had been drinking it.

The bus homewards was not much quieter. It had to wait at pubs on the way for customers to pour the last of the ale down their throats before they wallowed across and climbed aboard.

On the hill before the village a car came close up behind, and tried to overtake; but it was not able to venture past on the twisting road. It had to wait in the village, too, when the bus stopped to let Dick and Bob out. It, like the bus, was full of lads. When the bus moved it moved too, whirring close up behind it and peering along its side.

It did not pass the bus there, however, but stopped in the middle of the village, reversed, and stopped again by Bob.

Mick pulled back one of the windows. "You know what I told you to do," he said, with a big beery belch.

"So why don't you . . ." But there his friends pulled him in to stop him shouting the next word, because they guessed it was one that might be complained of. The window closed, and the car shot off down the road again, but came to a stop in front of the village hall at a funny angle. The engine stopped and the lights went out, the horn blew, and the lights went on, a door opened, and slammed again, the engine roared once more, and there was a spinning of wheels and a crunch, because the car had run into the village hall. There was a reversing again, and a tinkling of glass, and the car was blind in one headlamp. To make up for it a foglamp came on and glared a bilious ginger on the wall of the next house.

"They're full," said Dick. "Me, I'd rather have a cup of tea."

He climbed on to the seat of the tractor, switched on, pushed the gear lever to start, and lit the single lamp at the front. Bob settled his feet on the towing bracket, and his hands on the mud-guards, and they set off up the lane.

It was not the darkest of nights, in spite of a cover of cloud. But it was too dark for Bob to see, he thought, what he could see: his own shadow on Dick's back. He turned his head and looked back down the lane. In the mouth of it was a car with one headlamp and a fog-lamp. The two little suns faded away, were filaments glowing, and were nothing. Dick had seen the light too; but he said the car was just turning round.

The tractor rattled up the lane. The hole in the exhaust system began to blare at them. Bob put one foot carefully down beside the axle and kicked the loose tin that was a cover for the hole further along, and reduced the noise.

He was aware of something behind him. The shadows and shapes and light thrown by the tail lamp of the tractor on the wall of the lane had changed; or the back-cast from the road on to Dick's back had changed. He guessed what it was, and without looking spoke into Dick's ear.

"They've come up behind us with no lights," he said.

"They're all as drunk as louses," said Dick, without looking back. "I know what, you hold on tight, and I'll go down to the gill and across it, and if they follow they'll get water in the engine, and we'll go round the fields and back the other way. Don't get shaken off. Who are they?"

"That one that spoke is Chapman," said Bob. "We had a bit of a shout this afternoon at his place."

"Top of Vendale?" said Dick. Bob said it was. "You been hearing about that business?" said Dick. "I don't know what it is, but it wants forgetting, that. They're a rough lot up there."

Then they turned off the lane leading to Ravensgill and went steeply down the side of the gill towards the water, and into the water and out the other side, with Bob riding the bucking back of the tractor with sprung arms and legs. He looked back to see what had happened, but there was no need. Many yards behind a light sprang up, facing up the gill. The car had gone into the water, swung round so that it faced up-stream, and stopped. The headlamp went on, and then the fog-lamp.

"Stop a minute," said Bob. Dick switched the engine off and stood on the brake. They heard doors being opened and shouting going on; and the lights of the car wavered and died, and there was silence, except for a shouting of "Where are they?"

"Nobody drowned," said Dick. "We'll go on without lights, slow like." He switched the lamps of the tractor off, and put the gear lever to start. There was a grunt and a hiss and a whirr, and the sucking of the cylinders could be heard, but the engine did not start. Dick leaned over and put his fingers on a plug lead and pressed the starter again.

"Got ourselves wet too," he said. "We'll have to walk and all."

Then there was a sudden elfin light round them, darting about their heads and over the ground. It was one of the lads from the car, with a shielded torch, walking a spot of light over them.

Bob smelt them before he saw them. They smelt of beer, and they were very close. He heard them breathe, and he dodged away. Somebody hit him on the shoulder with a hard object, and he grabbed it. He found he had the torch. He switched it on and shone it over the enemy, and then turned it off. There were five of them, and they filled the lane behind the tractor, and two had got beside it, and surrounded them.

Dick went over the wall to one side, and Bob climbed the hot tractor and went over the other, and ran over the field. The cut grass was here, and he felt it rustle dry under his feet. It had improved through the night, he thought.

He dropped behind the tedder, parked with its five wire wheels like chrysanthemums in the air. He did not use the torch, because he could see without it. Mick and his friends could see too, he knew; but they did not know the ground.

They were coming towards the tedder. It was the only thing in the field besides the building where the hay was kept. Bob lay down flat behind the black tyres of the tedder and tried to look like hay.

But they saw him, or they thought they did, and since he was there it was the same thing. He had to get up and run, going off at an angle to where there was a slack place in the wall, easier to cross. He thought the best place to be was down by the beck, where there was more darkness and more sound.

He came by the tractor again, and found Dick sitting in the lane. "You all right, Dick?" he said.

"Nothing broken," said Dick. "Kicked me in the belly and knocked my glasses off. It's you they want most."

"We'll both get away," said Bob. "I've got their torch."

They heard the followers again. They had spread as they came across the field, and now they were climbing the wall at five separate points, pushing the top off to make the climb easier.

"You get away, Bob," said Dick. "I'll be unconscious if they come, because I can't see to do anything, and I haven't enough breath left to run with you."

Bob vaulted a gate and ran over a field clear of hay. Beyond it was the steep side of the gill, over the far wall, where the ground was rough and where disguising whin bushes grew.

The chase came after him. He crossed the wall, knowing where the wire was down. The followers found the wire and came through cursing. It occurred to Bob that if there had been no aggravation such as injuring their car, or letting them be caught in wire, there might have been no trouble. He crouched behind a whin bush. Two of the followers thought they saw him, and tackled a whin bush together. Bob had to put his thumb against the sharp edges of his teeth and bite, to stop himself laughing at them. Then they stopped cursing and began to put matches on the whin bushes. The dried prickles blazed like paraffin and then died down. When the flames are up there is plenty of light; and by that light they saw him, with four clumps of whin circling him. He covered his eyes from the light and ran down to the water, and turned up the beckside. Behind him the whin roared and spluttered, and against the light he saw them following him again.

It was not clear to him where he was going. When he had been on the tractor he had thought only of going home; but now home did not seem any better than anywhere else. If Dick was making his way home with a kicked belly and no glasses it might be best to lead this lot away. But he thought they might tire soon, and go away.

As they came they were striking matches and thrusting them into the whins, and leaving a bright trail topped with smoke. With this light they could sometimes see Bob, but it was no help to him, and hindered him from looking back to see how far ahead he was.

He clambered on, up the bed of the water at times, at other times along the side and now and then making an excursion to the top of the bank; but when he did that he showed against the sky too well. And at the top of the bank there was a wall with wire, so that he could not readily climb it before they caught up with him.

The chase went on. Fire glowed behind him again and again. He began to lose his breath. The torch was a nuisance. He thought of dropping it in the water. It was no use to him, because if he switched it on they would see him at once. He held on to it, and thought he might use it as a club. It was a rubber torch, with a plastic glass, and it was waterproof. He thought of lighting it before dropping it in the water.

Then he was at the earth dam, and the pool was ahead of him. He lit the torch then, gave a great breathless shriek, picked up an idle rock lying on the bank, and threw torch and rock into the pool, and ran away to one side.

They came up and stood on the bank. They talked among themselves and decided it was a trick, and said so loudly, and then they said they were coming to get him. They ignored the torch in the water. Bob was perched on the side of the hill now, open to view. He had not had time to go as far as he wanted, and now it was too late to move. Two of them came along the hill below him, and three of them went round the far side of the dub, climbed up beside the fall, crossed the water there, and came round to meet the others. They were all round him, and Bob stood up.

They mistook him for one of themselves, because they were too tipsy to be bothered to count. He walked with them down to the edge of the dub. One of them bent and lit a whin clump, and the light flared, coming back in molten ripples from the water and hanging in the fall.

They saw him then, among them. They were all round him. Bob went the only way there was, into the dub. There was a shout, and there was someone in the water with him. It was Mick, and now they were racing for the torch.

Bob got it, and turned it off. Mick swam away from him and began to shout: "Chuck summat at him, can you see him?"

Stones began to fall round Bob. He ducked under water, and one floated down against him, having lost its impetus entering the water.

He swam under water. Above him there was something that was the underneath view of the surface, wrinkling and negative, with a pattern that was fire but inside-out, and broken with inverted splashes where stones were coming in. Bob sunk himself and held on to a rock. He felt the pull of water, and he was taken against a shore and held there. His head came out of the water. He was under the overhang of a bank. To one side he heard the shouts of the followers, throwing stones at random. To the other side he heard the rumble of underground water; and he knew where he was: at the mouth of the channel he had been in before. He lifted himself on to the ledge the bars were fixed to, and found only a few inches of water. He dared a small flash of light, and saw where the gap in the bars was, and let himself through feet-first; and all the noise from outside went, and he was in safely; and not only in safety, but in much better order than when he had been in before, because he had a torch, and he knew where he was.

He was wet. When he first came through he had had an idea of waiting until daylight, in three or four hours' time; but he knew he must not sit wet in the cold tunnel for so long, because the combination of cold and wet would kill him. At the least he would have to keep moving about, and try not to be lost in any array of caves.

There was no array of caves. He was in a simple tunnel, and he could see easily, with the light of the torch, which was very powerful, that the tunnel was man-made, or had been adapted by man. He thought it might be something to do with lead-mining, a thing that Tot had often talked about. There were tool marks on the walls and roof, and in places along the side-walls there were wrought stones and masonry. The tunnel was straight, so that the thrown beam of the torch vanished ahead and only the walls gave a refracted and bare light: the darkness absorbed everything ahead.

There was no way of going wrong. He walked forwards, over a smooth and not even slippery floor. There was one step, down which he had been washed when he was last in here, and that was there deliberately. Otherwise there was a gentle slope, as imperceptible as the slope on the railway he had cycled up earlier in the day. Now though, he knew the slope was there because of the run of the water.

He walked down a hundred paces, and then back. It was no warmer. He went to the entrance and tried to listen out. He could see a glow of light, where there was another whin bush burning, but he could not hear sounds above the waterflow.

He turned and walked down again, this time going twice as far before pausing. Nothing had changed in the tunnel, and he thought that another hundred paces might bring something into view. He walked them, and there was still no change. Most important of all was the knowledge that there were no side tunnels at all, and no way of getting lost as he went up and down. His clothes began to dry from the dripping state to a clammy one.

There was more noise ahead now. Then the beam of the torch began to hit on rock straight ahead. He assumed he was coming to a corner; but it was not, when he came to it, a left or right turn, but a turn downhill. He was at the top of a waterfall under the earth, a man-made fall going down in regular steps. He stopped at the top, because this was far enough to go, he thought, and looked down. He was tired now, and he held on to something in the wall, as he looked down this rocky throat at the water breaking white, wondering whether the water was white even without light.

He was holding on to the rung of a ladder, one of the lower rungs. He flashed the torch round him, and saw that he was in a rounded place, where the walls were a different shape. He sent the beam upwards, and saw it touch on nothing near, but only on some cover to a deep shaft far above. The shaft itself, rising above him, had metal girders in it, and wood stagings, and was probably, he thought, part of the workings for when the tunnel was built. He wondered whether by going up he would be brought out of the underground place.

It was a stout ladder, going up like a staircase to a level of girders, along the side of the shaft. He went up the first few layers, and found the exercise warmed him. He let the torch look down once, from about forty feet, or four stages, and found that the depth did not look deep, because there was nothing to judge by.

He went on, climbing ladder after ladder, until he was quite out of breath; but he did not like to stop and let his wet clothes settle on him. He came to the top, where the sides closed in, and he saw how the girders below had made an internal framework to the shaft, stretching down from a square opening to the tunnel below.

Above him now there was a square frame with a stone closing it, and masonry arching in, and steps up the side of the arch. He climbed the steps and got under the flag. It was evidently a trapdoor of some sort, and he got his shoulders under it. He wondered whether he was in some old well that was under the floor of Ravensgill farm, and whether, if he got out through the trapdoor he would be in the kitchen, upsetting the cat. He pushed, and the flag lifted and stirred. He got tighter under and lifted again, and pressed unrelentingly so that the slab came up and grew lighter, because its weight was now not on him but on its own edge.

Then he balanced it, and stepped out.

He was not in the kitchen. He was between stone walls. At first he thought he was in some higher reach of the underground working; and then he knew he was in the bottom of the sighting tower on the edge of the moor. He caught the slab with his hands, having put the torch in the grass, and lowered it into its place, and kicked it down pretty level. Grass had caught under its edge, and it was not flat.

He put the torch out, and looked down towards the dub. He listened, unsure about the followers, who might have seen his light if they had been spread far from the dub on the other side of the gill.

He heard nothing there. But further down there was light, and he identified the light in a little while. It was the single headlamp and the foglamp of the car. He heard the motor spit into life, then die. In a little while it came again, and he heard it drive off.

He walked down to the house. Next he had to see about Dick. But Dick was in the yard, looking cautiously and blindly about.

"It's me," said Bob. "Have they all gone?"

"Yes," said Dick. "Grandma's having hysterics, Tot's locked himself in, and they've gone. One of them was sick in the yard, and they all pee'd against the back door, and they broke a window in the shippon, but that's all."

Grandma was sitting on the stairs in her nightie and coat. There had been tears in her eyes. "Bob," she said. "Have they hurt you? I knew it would never end. It will go on for ever; and it was their doing, not ours, always theirs. They would never believe me, you know, never. They blamed me, and it was all their doing, they turned him against us."

Dick came, blinking but calm. "Now Grandma," he said, "no harm done, just some drunk lads." Between them they took her up to her bed and put her in it. Bob went down and kicked the fire up a little and put the kettle on. It was still only half past ten, and a natural time for a cup of tea; but Grandma had gone to bed in her martyred and lonely mood, and only been woken when Dick had felt his way in and sat there holding his belly. After that the five lads had come and beaten on the door and shouted things that Grandma would not repeat and that Dick just shook his head about, when Bob asked them. Then they had done the things described, threatened to come again with a policeman and get them all locked up, and gone away. In a little while, before they had had time to start worrying over him, Bob had come in.

XV

MICK WOKE when Wig was manhandling the milkcans early in the morning. He got dressed in his working clothes, and then sat on his bed and thought for a time. Gran, in the next room, began to tap on the wall, irritating him to move. He stopped his thinking and went to Judith's room.

She said "Get out."

"Jude," he said, and stopped to cough a thickness from his throat.

"You stink of beer and fags," said Judith. "And your face is grey."

"I think I killed Bob White," he said. "We went up there last night, and I don't know what happened next. We were all fighting."

"They'll lock you up," said Judith, without thinking what a little phrase like that meant.

"I'll go and help Wig," said Mick.

When he had gone Judith leaned on one elbow and tasted the facts over again. They were simple: Mick had been to Ravensgill, and he thought he had killed Bob White; but they were not facts that stood alone. They carried with them another story and another set of facts, when some other person had gone to Ravensgill and had not come back. That made things even, and in a way fair. There was also the set of facts concerning the law and the set of facts, more important, about what Daddy and Mother and Wig and Gran, and even the two little ones, would think and say and do; and there was Mick himself, who was her own brother, who had become another like that elder White whose name she had never heard, whose name was never used in the house, or at Ravensgill, because of the thing he had done. Though Bob White said it was certain he hadn't.

Judith changed elbows and found she was now looking at the wall, and got up. Perhaps, she thought, Bob isn't dead yet, but lingering, and won't die. Or perhaps Mick only imagined he had been to Ravensgill.

She dressed in trousers and shirt, because it was not a school-day, and went to help Mother with the breakfast. The little ones got up like two little whirlwinds and went out into the sunshine to play. It was Sunday sunshine, that seems to be as hot as any other, but is not doing any work with its heat, because of the day.

Mick came in at breakfast time and said he was not very hungry, and went up to his room. Daddy looked at him and said nothing, and Mother carefully did not look at him. Gran said "Poor lad, you've been overworking," and Mick moved his mouth to show he was smiling and walked slowly upstairs.

"Hay fever," said Wig. "That's what."

"It'll cure," said Mother.

"Aye," said Wig. "I'm cured."

After breakfast Judith went up to look at Mick. He was lying on his bed asleep and pale. She sat on his bed for a little while, and wiped away a glister of sweat from his face. Then she heard someone at the door, and went down dreading the appearance of news from Ravensgill. It was only the milk lorry. If there was any news he would bring it, but he was not the more dreaded voice of authority. He, like the postman on weekdays, came for his cup of tea.

He had no fresh news with him; only the Sunday paper, which he brought up each week. Judith looked at the headline with impatience, knowing that it would say nothing about Mick and Bob White, but angry with it for not doing so. She went out to the implement shed and brought out her bicycle, and asked Mother whether she could take a ride on the lorry down to the village to see Christine Hammerton and be back in time for dinner. They might go for a little ride themselves on their bikes, she said.

She was rattled down the track among the cans, and dropped at the village. She went to Christine's house, but Christine was out already, gone strowing in a hayfield. Judith had to take her ride alone.

She remembered how the map lay, when she and Bob had looked at it in school. It had not shown the hills very well, but the actual world showed them very well indeed. Judith went down the valley, and then up the side of it, and down a hill that was ready to make her dizzy. She had walked up, and now she walked down. When she got to the village she asked the way, and was directed up a narrow lane, and she had to walk once more.

In the lane she came on broken glass, the side of a pair of glasses, a blood-stained rag, and a tooth.

*

Early in the morning Bob had gone out to look for Dick's glasses. He had found them with the lenses intact but one of the side pieces missing, in the lane by the tractor. There were large thumb and finger prints on the glass, and the side that was still on had been twisted and cracked.

The tractor was still standing where it had been left. Bob slipped the cover off the distributor and dried the inside with his handkerchief. He pressed the starter, and the engine turned and caught. He drove back to the house, and took the glasses in to Dick. Dick looked at them carefully. He could see things that were close to him.

"We'll have a bit of a mend," he said, and he threaded them up with wire and bound them to his head. Then he went to join Tot at the milking.

Grandma was still in bed. She had lain long awake, and now still slept. Bob lit the fire and put together a breakfast, and waited for Dick and Tot. As he waited he brushed soot from the back of the fire and watched it burn and smelt it. Some of it was caught up and went up the chimney. His fancy went the long dark voyage with it. Once, he thought, a letter on blue paper had gone up the chimney and out; and he supposed that soot was going out now, because there is an outlet to every chimney, the same way as there was an outlet through a shaft from the underwater, an outlet through the sighting tower.

Then he reasoned it out again, and found he had been wrong. He had come out of the tunnel through the sighting tower; but the water went on down an internal fall; and the water must come out somewhere, if the tunnel had been made by man.

Then he decided that the thought was inconclusive, because the tower and the tunnel were probably part of a lead mine, and the water had gone in accidentally, and was not meant to flow there at all. So to expect the waterway to go anywhere was nonsense. But all the same, his bathing trunks had got away from him in that same water, and they had come out in Vendale, being carried by all sort of chances clear through a multitude of narrow channels and grykes and swallows, to come out and be recovered and save him from paying the fine at the end of the school year.

In the middle of breakfast Grandma came downstairs. She was fighting depression with an aspect of dignity. She was frightened and brought low by the events of the night, and now she queened it to make up, and to keep memory away from her still.

After breakfast the royal mind turned to thoughts of housework and washing up; but only managed to get the pots to the sink, and then looked in the fire. She thought she was alone, but Bob was there and heard her mutter "he didn't do it," and he wanted to tell her that he knew that too; but without a proof of some sort there seemed little point in speaking. If he could prospect the shorter way over the Moss and Huker Mire then he could say something to comfort her. But he had not yet done it.

There was a knock at the door. Grandma assumed it was Tot wanting to be in, and she shouted to him. Bob thought it was Tot as well, because Tot and Dick had gone out, and Bob was about to follow, after eating more bread than either of the others. Dick was feeling sick when he ate, after being kicked in the belly.

Judith walked into the dark kitchen, and no one looked at her. She saw a white-haired woman (though the hair was tinted blue) sitting by the fire, and she saw someone else in the shadow against the wall. Then the silence, and the way no one turned to look, made her sure that it was a house of mourning, and that truly Mick had killed Bob.

Then there was another knock at the door. Tot had rapped this time, and not waited for an answer. He walked in, taking off his cap and showing his shining pale scalp.

"By," he said. "Two on 'em, well I nivver. By."

So then Bob and Grandma turned to see what was going on. They saw Judith standing there, out of breath, and Tot in the doorway. Judith had just convinced herself that Mick had done that deed of murder, and that there was nothing for her to do but turn round and go back home and wait for horror to unfold on the house, and for Mick to be taken away. So she was far into incurable tears before she saw Bob. She stood in the middle of the kitchen howling.

"Two of what?" said Grandma. "Who's this?"

"I don't know," said Bob, not recognising Judith at all with her tears and her hands at her face. He was trying to make her out to be one of the Gatestead girls; and Grandma was coming to the same conclusion, and had her hands on her hips ready to help her breathe as she laid into her with her tongue.

"Two of you, Lizzie," said Tot. "That's what it is, two of you. That's just how you were when you were a little lass; and this'll be a Chapman out of New Scar House."

"I thought it was a Gatestead," said Grandma. "But I was smaller than that, Tot, I was less across here," and she patted Judith's plump flank.

"Get off my bit of fat," said Judith. She was realising that nothing was wrong at Ravensgill—she could see Bob through tears—and she began to cover her crying with pretended rage.

"Oh, it's Judith," said Bob, knowing her now. "Are you looking for Mick?"

"No," said Judith. "I was looking for you. Mick said he thought he . . . he thought he . . ."

"Oh," said Bob, "not me, he couldn't."

"I'll go and tell him," said Judith. "Excuse me."

But she could not go then, because Dick came to the door. "Here," he said, "my glasses fell off again, and I've run over the bicycle, and I can't see a thing."

Bob went out to help, and saw a good red bicycle well crushed under the tractor, with the wired-up glasses hung in a bent spoke of the back wheel. He gave the glasses to Dick, who fixed them on again and surveyed the damage.

"Ours is a black bike," he said. "A bull bike too, and this is a little heifer."

"Judith Chapman," said Bob. "In the kitchen. Came to see if it was true Mick had killed me last night."

"She shouldn't have left it just between building," said Dick. "She'll have to walk back; but we can set her down to the village on the tractor."

"She bawling yet," said Bob. "And Tot flying round saying she's like Grandma when she was that age."

"Maybe that was when he started to fancy Grandma, when she was that age," said Dick.

"How do you mean?" said Bob. "Tot fancy Grandma?"

"Aye," said Dick. "Did you never know? That's why he

stays here never being paid. I don't suppose he bothers much now he's so old; but that's what kept him here all these years. He could have gone anywhere else and been paid."

"I never thought of it," said Bob. "Never came to mind."

Tot was walking about the kitchen, moving cups about, and saying "We must give her summat, she'll need summat." Judith was looking at him in a startled way, and still crying, but the crying was of a left-over running-down sort.

"What are you doing, Wig?" she said.

"I'm not Wig," he said. "I'm Tot. Wig's my brother. And I'm his," he added, to prove it. Then he went on laying saucers on the table.

"He doesn't know which he's courting," said Dick; and Grandma gathered up all the saucers again and sent Tot out of the kitchen, and he went smiling and muttering to himself, and took a rake out to one of the gill fields.

Judith gave a great sniff and sat on the table, then remembered her manners and got off it again. "What about my bike?" she said, because she had been out and looked and gone in again following Tot, when she thought he was Wig and a familiar thing.

"Busted," said Bob. "We can take you to the village on the tractor."

"Mick thinks," she started to say, with her voice clogging with tears again. "I'll have to tell him."

"It was just a fight," said Bob. "Let him worry a bit. We won."

"And I've come all the way for nothing," said Judith. "And he's still asleep in bed. Can I wheel my bike?"

There were some more tears when they were looking at

the bicycle. They said they were tears of grief at the damage done to the wheels, but they were still tears left over from the last crying. They dried up, and that spasm was over.

Dick and Bob thought they might manage something with the machine, and perhaps even made it rideable, but it would take a little time.

"You'll have to have your dinner here," said Dick. "Then you may be able to ride back, or push it."

Dick jacked up the tractor and pulled the bicycle out. Then while he looked at it Bob drove Judith down to the village, though she said she could have gone alone, and she telephoned home. She asked for Mick, and Mother sent him downstairs, and he listened to her while she told him that she'd come to Ravensgill and seen Bob, who was perfectly well and thought he had won the fight. Mick took the news very calmly, and did not even thank her. He gave the telephone back to Mother, and Judith told her she would be staying out for her dinner, because the bicycle was broken, and asked what Mick was doing. He was getting up, said Mother, and asking for food, the silly boy. He was that, said Judith, and added a goodbye.

XVI

ON THE way back up the lane Judith had Bob stop the tractor, and showed him the side of the glasses, and the bloodstained rag, and the tooth. They took the side piece home, and left the rest. Bob said the blood and the tooth were part of the enemy, he was glad to say; and he hoped it wasn't Mick's tooth, that was all.

The bicycle was repairing nicely. Dick was an expert hand at keeping doubtful machinery together and working, so he was an even better one at repairing an almost new thing. There was nothing for Bob to do to help. He and Judith walked round the buildings and looked at the calves. Then Judith fancied a look at the tower up on the hill, and the gill below. Bob said that he had escaped from Mick by way of the tower. Judith thought she would like to see what he had done. He borrowed Grandma's wellington boots for her (they were twins again in being the same size at the feet at least), and they walked up through the pasture and along the track.

"There's one of these in our land," said Judith. "Mick climbed up it once and saw another one on the top of the hill, where you can't go, you know, because of the Mire."

Bob said he had seen one from this tower; but that was not

the one Mick had climbed, because there were more than two of them, Tot had said.

He had brought the torch with him. He gave it to Judith to hold, and lifted the flagstone. It was so heavy now that he wondered at being able to move it last night. He got it on edge and dropped it over on its back. From below came the sound of moving water, a sound like wings on leaves.

"Down?" said Judith.

"Down," said Bob. "I'll go first."

Judith came slowly at first, and then quicker as she learnt how the ladder lay. Bob, shining the torch up for her to place her feet saw the square of light above shrink in size. It was not sky he saw, but a pure light falling down the shaft, thinning as it came.

Then he was in water, and it filled his shoes, and the torch showed the texture of it by his feet. Judith stood beside him, and they looked down the waterfall, and flashed the light down it as if they were tiny surgeons surveying the glottis of a giant.

Judith angled her watch into the beam of the torch. "A long time yet," said Bob. "I came from behind us last night, and it isn't very interesting. What if we go down this fall?"

"I dare," said Judith. "We could go on for half the time, and come back for the rest."

"Do you really dare?" said Bob. "It's cold, that's all."

"It'll go right to our tower," said Judith. "Then we could climb that and I'd be home."

Bob thought it was highly unlikely that the towers were connected by the tunnels, but there was no point in arguing. He really thought that they would go so far down the waterfall

155

and find the way blocked where the water filled the lead mine. He set off down the fall, and they walked side by side, because there was plenty of room and the water was seven inches deep only, though running fast.

The fall sloped less and less, and in a little while there were no more steps, but only the straight passage and the gentle slope. They walked on, and they walked, and the tunnel began to be wearisome, because it was endlessly the same. Then the sound changed, and the roof vanished, and they were walking in a channel cut in the floor of a cave. Overhead were curtains of stone, and to either side pillars of it, and a drip of water from the roof. They went into the familiar tunnel again, and the sounds closed tight round them, the echoes dying away.

There was another shaping in the walls, and they were at the foot of another shaft. The light climbed it, and did not reach the top.

"Go on," said Judith; and they walked on down the easy slope.

They struck another cave, and here there was an underground bridge to carry the water above the floor. They leaned on the damp edge of it and flashed the light round, to see what they could. There was a vault of stalactites, and a forest of stalagmites on the floor below, and the stone was coloured, brown and green and red, with white streaks and blue casts.

"Can we go there?" said Judith. "Would we get lost?" And her words cracked back as consonants and boomed back as vowels. Bob whistled, and the pipers piped back to him, as if the pillars hanging and standing were part of an organ that played only echo and not substantive sound.

"I've a bit of band," said Bob, bringing from his pocket the usual lengths of baler band that accumulates from straw bales and is saved for useful purposes.

He climbed out of the channel he was in and jumped down to the floor. There was loose rock here, and he anchored an end of the twine to a rock and perched it on the wall. Then he knotted ends together, and made a clew to draw them back to where they had been.

There was an obvious little pathway among the stalagmites, where someone had been sometime. There were marks, frosting over with lime again, where tools had worked through the jungle.

At the end of the pathway there was a clearing, and in the clearing was a wooden hut with a felt roof. The front of the hut was open, and in it was a table and two benches. In front stood a coke brazier, with coke still in it. On the table lay a broken plate, and on the back wall a calendar hung marked with an unidentifiable month in 1898.

They did not touch, but retraced their steps, going right back to the channel.

They looked in another direction, and saw only the growing stone, and no more huts. Then, in case by some accident they lost the way, they climbed back into the water, and walked on, because they were not halfway to their time yet.

There was another shaft rising at the end of the cave. The tunnel closed again, and they walked on. Bob thought of Staddle Hill above him with all its weight, and sent the thought away again. "Seventeen minutes more," he said. Judith nodded.

Nine of those minutes later they come to another rising

shaft, and they could see the top of that with the torchlight. They left it and went on.

Something went wrong with the torchlight. It faded, and grew less vivid. Perhaps the colour of the walls was changing, or the filament of the bulb had wearied. "Hold on," said Bob. "We don't have to worry because we can feel our way, but it's going strange." He flicked the torch off and on, and off again. And they could still see where they were going, because there was a bluish light ahead, changing, as they came closer to it, to a green light, and then to a strong yellowy red.

There were bars in front of them, and daylight, and the end of the tunnel. They came to the bars and looked through, and saw a sheet of water. Bob had confused ideas about Australia being in a downward direction, though the other way up. But this lake was the right way up.

"Hey, White," said Judith. "This is our rezzy, and that's the dam, and that's our chimneys there. We came through the hill."

"Then that's how he did it," said Bob. "That's how he was over here in Vendale at one time and back so soon at Ravensgill, because he didn't come over the top and he didn't go by the road, he came through here, and it took us an hour and we don't know the way and we looked at things as we came."

"Oh yes," said Judith, "but let's get out."

"We're going back for our dinner," said Bob. "Aren't we?"

"Not if I can get through," said Judith.

"I can't, you can't," said Bob, thinking these bars would be the same as the ones at the other end. But they were not so closely set, and he was able to push through and stand out in fresh air.

"Help me," said Judith. "I can't get. Don't go away, I don't want to go back, I don't like it in here any more."

"I'll give you a pull," said Bob; but a pull was no help.

"I'm all right till my hips," said Judith. "Your Lizzie was right, I am too fat. Why don't you shout for help?"

There was no need to shout for help, because Mick, lounging on the dam, had seen movement in the big grating in the base of the retaining wall against the hill. He came quickly over the dam, crossed the fence, and along the contour of the high-water mark.

"Help me, Mick," said Judith. "I can't get out."

"What did you put her in there for?" said Mick. Bob had an idea of explaining, then abandoned it, because there was fighting in the air. Neither of them took any more notice of Judith, except to put the torch near her, which Bob did, vaguely supposing that she might need it to go back up the tunnel if they had to go on fighting beyond the fixed going-home time. Then he had his jacket off, and handed it to Judith. She took it, and Mick's, and they were ready to fight.

"Fair do's," said Mick. "No biting or kicking or belly-fouling."

"Winner's the one still living," said Bob.

It was a big fight, mostly in the gully of the stream where it flowed down to the reservoir. Some of it was on the rocks beside the gully, and part of it was in some thick black mud lying in a flat place. After that they were in the water again, and they lost all the mud, and a shoe from Mick's foot. Then they rested, because that round had lasted ten minutes.

Judith was still in the tunnel, holding the coats, and shouting at them both, always urging the one on top to hit a bit harder. She went on shouting at them when they rested, but they had forgotten her. During the second round she dropped both jackets in the water, tried to get through the bars again and became wedged, then forced herself back in and tried at a different angle, lying on her side and trying to swivel round the bar instead of going through them upright.

She was helped by the two little ones, who came down to see what was happening. They pulled and pushed, and darted in and out of the tunnel mouth and made their socks muddy.

The two fighters began to find something was interfering with the fight. It was Wig, who was persistently combing them apart with a hayrake, and being rough with it too. Bob shouted at Tot for it, because both old men were so alike. Mick shouted at Wig; but for neither of them would he stop. Wig reversed the rake, and instead of using the teeth to divide them he used the handle to batter them. Neither of them could fight with two opponents, and they drew apart.

"Now, that's plenty," said Wig. "It'll do."

"Who won?" said Mick.

"Nobody," said Wig. "There isn't a winner between two jackfools, they're both fools, that's all."

"It's a fight to death," said Mick; but before he could start again Wig gave him a hefty twilt with the shank of the rake, and a tooth came out of the rake. Mick stopped offering to fight.

Judith went home. She had had enough of both of them. She took the little ones with her, and left the combatants and the peacemaker by the water.

"We've stopped," said Mick. "Haven't we, White?"

"Is he one of them?" said Wig. "He has the look."

"No worse for it," said Bob.

"I know who he is, Wig," said Mick. "It was his grandfather killed my great uncle."

"Abram," said Wig. "Abraham rightly. If it wasn't for what Lizzie said, but then she'd be bound to."

"You didn't believe her," said Bob. "Because you thought he couldn't have got over in the time. But what's the time now?"

Wig looked at his watch. He kept it in his purse. He told Bob the time, and Bob told him that an hour ago he was in Ravensgill with Judith.

"Yes, she telephoned," said Mick. "And then who brought you?"

"We came through there," said Bob, pointing to the barred exit. "It runs straight to Ravensgill."

"Nay," said Wig. "That never shows but in a dry summer; but it was a dry summer that year, it was dry. And can you get out yon end?"

"In and out," said Bob. "Easier than this."

"There's always summat new," said Wig. "Well, I doubted Lizzie, I will say, and I couldn't see any other way; but if it's right what you say, then I'll no doubt no more, and no more will others."

"I've got to get back," said Bob. "To my dinner. And then I'll bring Judith's bike over in a bit. When you broke Dick's glasses they wouldn't stay on, and he never saw the bike; but he's fettling it now."

"You'd best come to the house," said Mick. "You'll not be wanting to be back in those wet clothes."

"And your Judith's got our Grandma's boots on," said Bob.

"Away then," said Mick. "Cousin."

"We'll —— off," said Bob. "Eh?"

Mick had to try his lungs in the big cave, with vulture cries and vampiring. Meanwhile Bob found the rock with the baler band on it, and pulled the wet string between his fingers. They had a torch each now, and a paraffin lantern, the kind with a mantle that gives a light like a street lamp. Mick gave it a pump or two and set it on the parapet. They left it there as a lighthouse, and followed the clew.

Bob took him to the hut first, and they wondered at the builders of the tunnel, so many years ago, living like cavemen in the cave they must have found by chance. Then they tracked about among the folds and galleries of the cave wall. They found the head of a hammer, and small coil of rope that was turning to stone as the water seeped through it.

Below another ledge there was something that glittered and winked. It was a gold coin, with Victoria on one side and a horseman on the other: there was the deposit of lime on it that was on everything. Then they found another, and then a little heap, with the metal uncorrupted, and only a coat of stone that could often be wiped off.

There was a mass of rusty metal, two loops with a chain between. Bob stirred it, half recognizing what he had found. One loop came up, flaked with decay. With it came some small white stones that fell lightly down again.

They were bones. They were the bones of a hand; and in the other loop lay the separated wrist bones of another hand, and the arms were beyond, and the skull, clean and round and

grown to the floor with the settling water, and beyond the skull the backbone, the worn spoons of the pelvis, a broken thigh bone and its whole fellow, and the lower bones of the legs. In the manacled grasp of the skeleton Bob saw a small thing that was gold but not a coin, and hung on a tiny failing fingerbone a ring; and these he took, for Grandma; and this was her husband. And he took the manacles, the handcuffs that had been put on him.

XVII

"Auntie Lizzie," said Mick. "I came on to say I was sorry about last night, and all that."

"You should be," said Grandma, "if that was you, whoever you are."

"My Gran is your cousin," said Mick.

"Chapman, you'll be," said Grandma. "Where's that little lass we had a bit since?"

"I took her home," said Bob.

"You're a fool to go on the road with the tractor," said Grandma. "There are laws about it, and about passengers on them, and I don't know how often I haven't told you."

"It's all right, we walked," said Bob. "And Mick's come for his dinner instead."

There was a tap at the door, and it was Tot. Dick was behind, saying "She can try it now if she wants. It should go."

"We've had a change," said Tot. "We've a lad now, not a lass."

"Mick," said Bob.

"You've some funny friends, like," said Dick.

"We've got all settled now," said Bob. "And now wait on, here's a few things."

The first thing he found in his pocket was the thing that was gold and not a coin. It was a locket. He laid it on the table, and Grandma picked it up. "I know it," she said, and she nipped it with her thumbnails, and it sprang open. Inside was a little picture painted hard on ivory.

"Judith," said Mick and Bob together. Tot fumbled for his glasses.

"Me," said Grandma. "That your Grandfather had. I didn't know you had it over there. Why is it wet?"

The next thing was the ring. Bob rolled it on the table, and Grandma picked it up, ran a finger round inside it, and looked there. "The letters are too small," she said. "Is it E.W., C.W.?"

"Yes," said Bob, when he had had a look.

"Our wedding ring," said Grandma. "He said he would keep it until we met again, or it would come to me if he died. I know he's dead. If he hadn't been he would have come long since. But they didn't hang him. Why have you never told me, you Chapmans and Oldersbys?"

"We found these today," said Bob. "Before that there was nothing to tell. But there's some more things."

He put down the rusty handcuffs, and rusty spikes fell on the cloth.

"It was lamplight that time," said Grandma. "And when they put them on I went down in a faint, and that policeman brought some brandy out of the cupboard and poured it on my tongue while my man got away. Now if you go in that cupboard under the stairs, Bob, and up on the back shelf there's a flat bottle. That's it, and it's the same bottle, and you'll rinse a glass off the top shelf there, and I'll taste again." Bob rinsed the glass, drew the cork, and Grandma tasted again. Then she poured the rest back into the bottle and tasted no more, just smelling the glass.

"That was my father's," she said. "And now I've seen these things again, where is the one that's dead?"

"In the water tunnel under Staddle Hill," said Bob.

"Aye," said Tot. "And he might be at that; but I never dared think of venturing in, nor sending others."

"In, is he?" said Grandma. "I thought he had been lost on the tops, in the mire. Is there a way for a man through the hill?"

"Will he be to fetch out?" said Tot.

"No," said Mick. "It's bones now, and they're fast down with lime."

"Do you know where?" said Tot. "Because there's summat if you do, out here."

He led them outside, and paced about the yard. Then he tapped a flagstone with his foot. "This one," he said. "It wants to be up."

Bob thought that another tunnel was to be revealed, perhaps the one he had imagined himself to be in the night before and coming up in the kitchen. This was only a few feet from the kitchen, and not a bad guess.

Dick levered the flag up. Below it were worm and insect galleries and the pale roots of grass. Tot walked over to the shippon and brought a bucket of water. He did not pour it where Bob thought he would, into the hole where the stone had been, but on to the underside of the stone itself, and scrubbed it with the yard brush. They saw the lettering of an inscription emerge, clear and new and unread. "Beneath this place lies the body of Clifford Patrick White," and going on with the date of his birth and the date of his death. He was twenty-one when he died.

"He must ha' died then," said Tot. "Or he'd've been back, because he never did it. I know more about it than would be told in court or anywhere, but they never asked me. I know that Abraham came over to kill him, and was certain sure to, and I came over to stop him. He found out they were wed, ye see, and it rancoured him. I followed over, and he knocked me down and I thought I was dead, and then next thing is he was dead himself. He came to catch him in the tunnel under the hill, and finish it there. But the water was too much for him."

"Yes," said Bob. "I know where he went and how it happened, because it happened to me too."

"I don't know what it was," said Grandma, "but you both had the same marks."

"We'll get this stone up in the winter," said Tot. "One of these winters, and if we've to wait then we'll wait."

Tot dropped the stone down again, and they went in. Grandma was for having dinner now, because her sip of brandy had edged her appetite. But Bob had one more thing to show, and that was his pockets, and Mick's pockets, full of sovereigns.

"There's a hundred and fifty and three," said Grandma. "And they belong to me, and I gave him them that night in a leather bag; and he said he would get some more he had."

There were one hundred and seventy eight sovereigns and twenty three half sovereigns.

"It is the buried talent," said Grandma, "added to the

miraculous draft of fishes that brake the net." She took all the coins and put them in the big teapot and set it back in its dust on the dresser.

In the afternoon of the next day Bob was met in the village by a ginger-haired woman, who took him by the arm. It was about a minute before he fully recognized Grandma. She had on a clean new coat, new shoes, and the extraordinary reddish hair.

"Come on," she said, while he still blinked at her. "I waited for you." She took him to a taxi from Garebrough which was waiting outside the village hall. The taxi drove up to Ravensgill. In the kitchen waited Dick and Tot, both dressed up well, and with their hair smoothed back. Dick was peering about him, short-sighted. Grandma brought his glasses with a new frame from her new handbag, and he put them on. She sent Bob upstairs to change into a clean shirt. Then she led them all out to the taxi, and they drove away again.

They came to Vendale, and up the railway track to New Scar House. Grandma said she would walk over the dam, and when she was over the taxi could catch up. She wanted to feel the approach again, she said.

They drove up the last few yards of lane, and the taxi turned in the yard. Grandma got out, walked to the back door, and into the house.

"This end of the house belong to me," she said. "So don't you hoity-toity with me, Maggie."

Judith's Gran, Mrs Oldersby, or Maggie, looked at her cousin.

"You've had your hair dyed," she said. "If it isn't one thing it's another with you. And who's that? Tottie Tuker. Well you haven't changed."

"It's grand to see you, Maggie," said Tot. "I'll go and find Wig, and we'll have a bit of a crack; and I'll show you two lads about the place."

Grandma would not let them go. They were visiting, she said, and Tot could go where he liked, but her grandsons would stay where they should be.

"Margaret's just out in the field," said Gran.

"That's your girl, then?" said Grandma. "Well, how do you find yourself?"

"There's Mick outside," said Dick. "We'll go and talk to him." But they had to be introduced first to their great-aunt. They left the two old ladies facing each other either side of the fire, not sure whether there was to be a battle.

Tot had found Wig. Now, in the field below the house, where the hay was windrowed and being swept up, there were two old men instead of one, raking after the sweep.

Judith came out of the house. "Your boots are in the porch there," she said. Then she went in and lay on her bed to do her homework. Now she knew what the fuss had been about, and it was apparently over, she wondered why she had ever been agitated about it at all. If it had been forgotten and left alone, then the next generation would never have heard of it, nothing would have come to light, and the wound would be healed. She remembered that she had been told that very thing several times. She drew a ring round a page number in the history book, and added arms and legs and a head and called it Tot; and did the same to the facing number, and called it Wig. With them to watch she settled to the Industrial Revolution.

Downstairs two old ladies stopped talking. After more than forty years apart neither of them had anything startling to tell the other; and those whom one remembered the other had forgotten. In a little while no one was speaking at the top end of Vendale. All were busy with work or thoughts. Even the two little ones, for a long time, sat in the hay and said nothing.

XVIII

Tot had taken up the flagstone before winter, and stored it in the stick shed under the cowlings. Now, with a foot of snow crisp on the ground, he brought it out again, and laid it on the hay sledge. With it he put two shovels and an axe.

He blew on his hands. The horse, Dinah, licked its front leg and shivered, and its coat stood out a little.

"It doesn't like it outside so well," said Tot. "Now, have you those measures handy?"

"I wrote them down," said Bob. "And Mick will be there."

Grandma, with her parti-coloured hair, because the ginger of six months ago had grown out an inch and a half and not been brought up to date, came out in her long winter coat. She pulled a bobble cap over her head, put her hands in her pockets, and was ready. Bob went ahead and opened the gate into the lane.

"We should have a rocket to tell them we're off," said Dick. "What if they come on a different day?"

"No matter," said Tot. "There's only Wig that knew him of all that lot."

The horse led them up the lane. This was the way they had come for cowlings. Now the heather was under snow. The tower at the end of the track was the cause of a drift that rose eight feet across the centre gap. Beyond the tower was the plateau of Staddle Moss and Huker Mire, unfenced, unwalked, unused.

"We'll go till we see it," said Tot. "I hope it's frozen as hard as I think, because if not we'll be losing the horse."

This time of year was the only one when it was safe to wander on the Moss or the Mire. The ground had frozen hard before the snow came. It had lifted the flags outside the back door so that it would not open, and they had had to use the front door for more than a month.

The horse walked heavily. The shell of frozen vegetation and peaty mud vibrated under its feet.

"If it goes we'll all go," said Dick.

The second tower came in sight. The ground up here looked level, but it was not. There were ridges and slacks, and even some rock showing here and there. The towers could not have been built or their sites approached if there had not been some firm ground. The higher ground was the firmer.

"It begins to smell like a thaw," said Tot. "And I don't reckon there's snow in those clouds."

"They're thundercaps," said Grandma. "Over Vendale. It was always a more thundery place than Ravensgill."

There had been no wind; but now it began to blow from the West. It changed, and came from the east, and then cast about and came from any direction. Bob was sure he felt different winds at the same time on either ear.

"It's darkening," said Tot, naming what everyone knew. But it was early for darkening. Overhead more clouds were forming to join with the Vendale thundercaps.

The top of the snow began to glisten with damp. A sort of

sickly wind began to blow, heavy and hot, as if from some sour oven. Then there was rain, cooling the wind.

They came to the second tower, and ahead they saw the third, with people coming towards them over the snow. It was a long way to them, and though they would meet towards the middle and the distance was closing twice as fast as either party walked, the gap seemed to stay the same size.

There was a dip, and they lost sight of the others, and of the towers. Then they came up again, with difficulty through a massy drift with a hard and abrasive crust. Ahead were the others, Mick and Judith and Wig.

"We have to go right to the tower," said Bob. "We measured from the shaft of it."

"You go on and do it," said Tot. "Then we shan't need to trail so far."

Mick had done that particular work, though, and made Judith stand behind the tower and line up the next one, which it was easy to do with this pair, and keep him on the line. She had kept him on it, and he had paced the course of the underground bridge in the cave below, and then struck off the correct right angle the right distance, and come to the place that was directly above the skeleton. There he had dug the snow out with his hands to the frozen peat beneath.

Tot and the horse came up and stood. Tot brought out the axe and began to dig with it, carving his way into the frozen mass.

"It may never stand the summer," he said. "But it won't wander far. It's well heughed to the fellow now, with his name and hornburn on him like. All it can do is go down to him. But we'll set it upright for now."

Before he had finished digging the thunderstorm had begun, cracking the clouds a couple of miles higher up the ridge. The yellow lightning licked and skidded like the flame of spirit, blue in reflection, over the ridge of snow, picking the towers out black against the busy blue cloud.

Tot carved a neat trench for the stone, and they lifted it from the sledge and stood it on end.

"God have mercy on an innocent man," said Wig, and he trod frozen chippings in to hold the stone upright.

Then the rain came on them, cold rain that was yet warmer than the snow, and melted it and carved channels in it. In the rain the electricity flashed and circuited, and over the hissing sound of it was the earth-shaking thunder.

"We'd best get away sharply," said Tot. "It's not so very bad your side, but ours has some bad places."

They walked homewards, very cold. The snow was soft now, wet, very slippery, and the ice below was holding the water. Every low place was filling with water, or running with it; and the big drift on the bank was a mixture of water and snow, knee deep, and the sledge was awash.

All at once they came out of the thunder, into a cooler and drier air, and the snow below was firm again. Their coats began to freeze, and a blue darkness began to rise out of the valley towards them. Behind them the thunder rumbled, and they heard the water in the gill rising and rumbling, because water was coming off the hill.

"Don't put me at the top there," said Grandma. "And don't put me over here. Put me over in Vendale when my time comes, and not too near Maggie, we don't agree any more."